WHEN HE BECKONS

HALLI STARLING

Copyright © 2022 by Halli Starling.

All rights reserved. Printed in the United States of America. No part of this book may be used or reproduced in any manner whatsoever without written permission except in the case of brief quotations embodied in critical articles or reviews.

This book is a work of fiction. Names, characters, businesses, organizations, places, events and incidents either are the product of the author's imagination or are used fictitiously. Any resemblance to actual persons, living or dead, events, or locales is entirely coincidental.

For information contact : http://www.hallistarling.com

Book design by Halli Starling

Cover design by Halli Starling

ISBN: 979-8-9870048-1-4 (paperback)

ASIN: B0BCH9LXMZ (Kindle ebook)

First Edition: December 2022

10 9 8 7 6 5 4 3 2 1

Contents

Praise for Halli Starling's Books	V
Dedication	VII
1. Chapter 1	1
2. Chapter 2	7
3. Chapter 3	13
4. Chapter 4	20
5. Chapter 5	28
6. Chapter 6	34
7. Chapter 7	40
8. Chapter 8	53
9. Chapter 9	66
10. Chapter 10	72
11. Chapter 11	79
Acknowledgments	90

About Author

PRAISE FOR HALLI STARLING'S BOOKS

Praise for *Wilderwood*

"Starling's novel...will shatter readers' expectations with its bewitching complexities... [her] characters are provocative and engaging. Bellemy Eislen is equal parts intriguing and vulnerable, while Octavia Wilder easily fills the role of a well-defended, tenacious heroine."- ***The BookLife Prize***

Praise for *Ask Me For Fire*

"If you're a fan of deep personal stories, loners, neighbors to friends to lovers, mysteries, and two sweet guys finding their person this is the book for you." – ***Goodreads Reviewer***

"This was just gorgeous. A pitch-perfect slowburn romance, wonderfully atmospheric, perfectly paced, with a hint of suspense and some of my favourite tropes, expertly used." – ***Goodreads Reviewer***

For Agu, who inspired Deacon

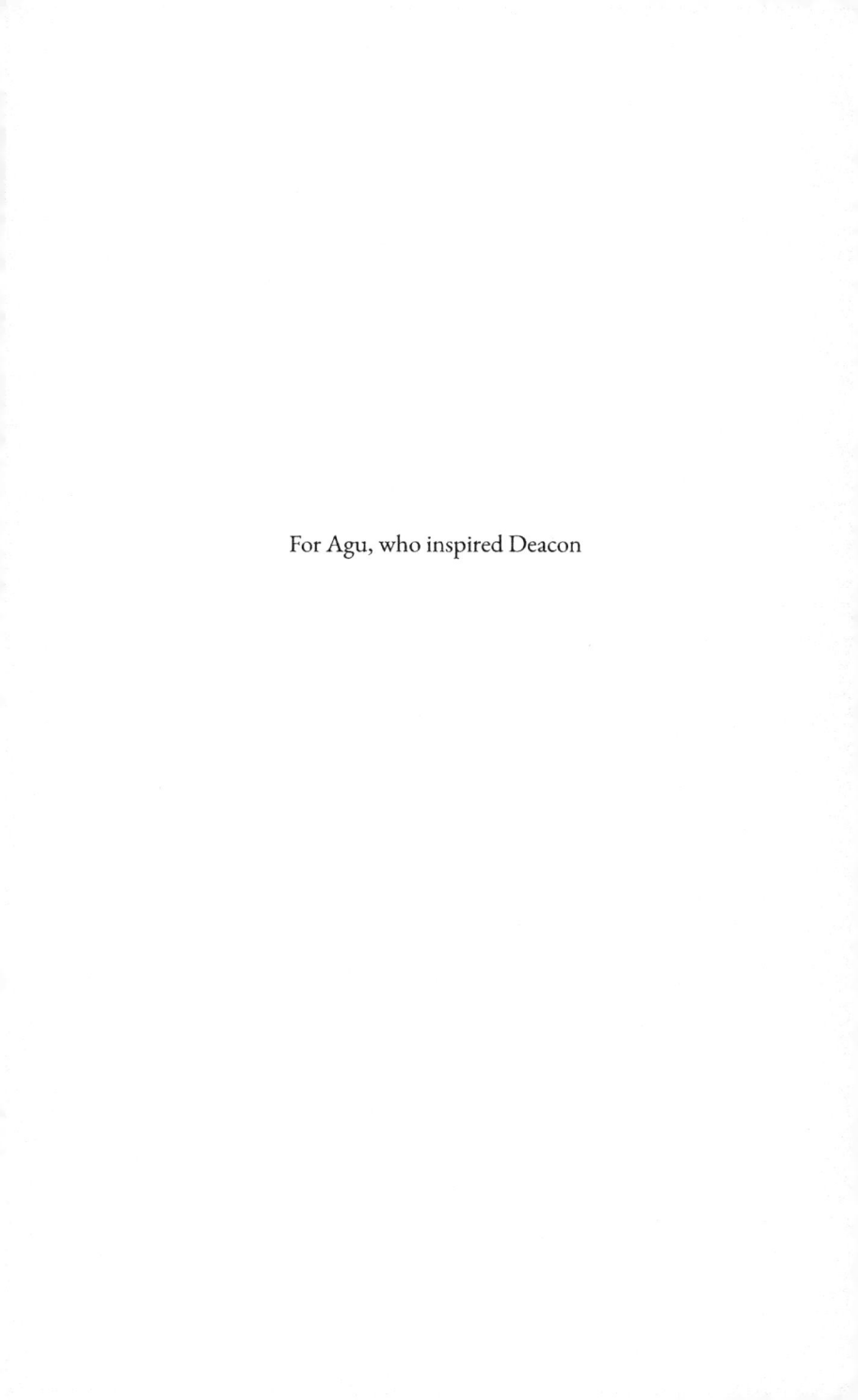

One

"Nice wheels."

Zan slowly lowered the sweating water bottle from his lips and squinted against the sun to find the source of the voice. He'd pulled over on this side of the bike trail because of the shade cast by glossy purple maple leaves. He also liked stopping at this point on the trail to watch the skateboarders, the sound of their wheels *snicking* against concrete oddly soothing. But today he'd found the skate park eerily quiet. Sure, it was a Wednesday midafternoon a few weeks after school had gone into session, but Zan had figured there'd be someone sliding up and down the curved banks of concrete.

Instead, he was staring at the lone figure sprawled out on the uppermost skate ramp. *Lounging* was maybe a better word. The man's posture spoke of utter ease and apparently thick skin, since he was leaning back on his elbows with nothing to protect him from the concrete's bite. He was also dressed unlike any skater Zan had ever seen, in deep black leather pants, a red shirt that rose up to show a strip of tawny skin, and a bright yellow lily tucked behind his ear. The sides of his head were shaved close, but the thick black hair on top of his head was threaded with gray and pulled up high into a bun. And he was sporting a few days' worth of stubble along a pointy jaw, a thick leather cord around his neck, and a scatter of tattoos up and down his arms.

There was no skateboard in sight.

"Thanks," Zan finally said, a hint of caution in his voice.

"Yeah, sure." The man grinned. "The flames are a nice touch." He pointed to the hand painted red and orange flames along the body of Zan's bike. "Much nicer than that weird teal bikes get painted with all the time. Boring."

Zan had to snort at that. He felt the same. Plus painting his bike had been a nice way to spend a rainy afternoon. "Well, I always wanted a cool bike as a kid but never got one. And now..."

"You have one. Fuckin' ace, man." The man got to his feet and without a single look down, hopped off the high ledge and began walking over. He kept his distance, though, and said, "I'm Deacon."

Zan put out his hand, which Deacon took. "Zan. Nice to meet you."

"Yeah, yeah. You, too." Deacon ran brown eyes over Zan's sweaty bike gear, then gave an approving nod. "Biking's cool. You can go fast and be outside." He motioned to the skate park. "Skating's good, too, but you can only go so far, you know?"

Zan didn't want Deacon to think he was laughing *at him*, but the other man's easy posture and slightly unique way of speaking had him grinning. There was something magnetic about the guy that instantly drew him in; like Deacon had a life's worth of wild stories, even if he appeared to be only around forty. Maybe it was the playful twist to his lips, or whatever aura Deacon exuded. "Yeah, I get it," he said before taking another swig from his water bottle. "When I want to go fast, I bike. And when I want to take my time, I get out in the canoe."

"Shit, that sounds awesome." Deacon patted his right hip. "I nearly took my own hip off years ago, had it replaced. Now I'm part Iron Man or some shit, so I can't skate anymore. Canoeing I haven't tried though. That's a good thought." And then Deacon took the lily from his hair and handed it to Zan. "I gotta get before my employees start texting me but here."

Zan took the flower but felt awkward holding it aloft. "Uh, thanks."

Deacon shrugged, the move making the loose neck of his shirt slip down a little, revealing the edge of more tattoos. Zan was instantly curious. "No problem. Zan. It's a good name. A good name for a man on a cool bike. Be seein' ya." He jammed his hands into his pockets and walked off, headed for the sidewalk that would lead back into town.

"Bye." Baffled, Zan watched Deacon walk away. The flower was still in his hand when his smartwatch buzzed. It was his day off but like usual, someone at work needed something and it simply couldn't wait. Zan sighed, put the lily in his shirt pocket, and hopped back on his bike. All the way home he wondered who the hell he'd just met.

"So, it's done?"

Zan held back on a scream of frustration. He'd long lost track of the number of times he'd walked the office assistant through this *very simple reporting process*. A process that literally took five minutes and clicking on a handful of commands. But for whatever reason, Teny didn't get it.

Teny. Full name Tennyson Batchelder. Nice kid, always on time, always neatly pressed in a button-down shirt and slacks. But fully incapable of doing even the simplest task (like doing this *fucking report*). And Zan had no ability to fire him because Teny was the owner's nephew. Rucker Batchelder was a decent enough guy to work for, but his love of nepotism had caused Zan and several others in the office innumerable headaches over the years. Reporting was a backbone of their printing business and Zan was in charge of that process and so many others. Doing the job of a business analyst, head of sales, and sometimes marketer meant he was getting all kinds of great job experience...for shitty pay.

Zan saw the grimace on Teny's face and let out a deep breath. It wasn't the kid's fault he'd been raised to think the sun shone out of his ass, but learned helplessness was a thing. If Teny kept on this path, he'd soon start weaponizing that same helplessness. That never ended well.

"Hey, Teny," Zan said as he sat down at Teny's left, "would it help if I made a video for you about this? Just a recording of my screen and me walking you through these steps? Nothing against it, but I don't think the written instructions are working."

Teny gave a sad smile. The kid wasn't incapable of learning. Zan had witnessed progression himself. So maybe it was the process behind the learning. Hell, anything was worth a shot at this point. "Maybe? I know you wrote out these nice instructions," and he plucked up the laminated sheet near his right elbow, "but I'm just stuck."

The wobble in Teny's voice struck a chord in Zan's heart. Ah, shit. *Please don't cry.* "Hey, no worries. You watch me do the report this time, and by end of the week I'll have that video for you. Okay?"

"Yeah. Yeah." Teny perked up a little at that. "I'll get it, I swear."

And like always, Zan immediately felt bad for his own frustration. Teny wasn't really suited for an office job and everyone at Oakside Printing knew the twenty-one year old had struggled to find work that fit his talents. He was what Zan's nanna would have called "cloud-headed". Always dreaming up things, feet never tethered to the ground. Zan didn't think much of his nanna's choice of words most of the time, but Teny certainly fit that particular description. The kid was brilliant with words - Zan had read some of his work online when he couldn't sleep and was enough Scotch in to think it was a good idea to snoop around. But this office thing just wasn't his gig.

His watch buzzed. Rucker's text was simple: *Need you in the meeting room.*

Dammit. And on his day off. The report would have to wait.

"Tell you what," Zan said as he gave Teny a pat on the shoulder. "Head home. I've got this."

Teny's dark green eyes went big. "I can't. Uncle Rucker said -"

"I can handle your uncle. Go on." *Come on kid, go be twenty-one for once.*

Teny glanced at the computer, frowned, then nodded and got to his feet. "Thanks, Zan. You uh...." Teny's gaze landed somewhere near Zan's short beard. "I know I'm bad at this. I know I shouldn't be working here. It's hard to say no to Uncle Rucker on a good day." He twisted his hands together and the sight made Zan's heart clench painfully. "You've been really patient with me so I just wanted to say thank you." His narrow face brightened. "I put out twenty applications yesterday."

"That's great, Teny. I'm proud of you." Ah shit, this kid was going to break him with those puppy dog eyes and sad smiles. "You've got this. But I gotta..."

"Yeah, I know. Thanks."

Day off my ass, Zan thought as he jogged past the rows of cubicles and into the east hallway. The meeting room, which was really just a room filled with shitty chairs that bit into your back and a battered table Rucker had picked up at a yard sale, was at the end of the hall. The door was ajar and he heard Rucker's telltale boom as the man said, "Well, whatever your project, Oakside can get it done, Mr. Essex. We've printed everything from -"

"From biographies to birding guides, maps to magazines," Zan finished under his breath before knocking. "You called, Rucker?"

"Yeah, get in here. Now, Mr. Essex, I'm about to introduce you to the head of our printing business. He's the best there is and he'll do right by you and your customers."

"Hopefully my authors, too. Since there's no business without them."

Zan knew that voice. Had heard it only a few hours ago, rumbled out from a man with long black hair shot through with grey, a yellow lily tucked behind his ear. The lily now sat in a bud vase on Zan's kitchen windowsill. He stuck his head in and saw Rucker hip-up on the table, grinning down at the man seated to his right.

"Well, hello there," Deacon said when he spotted Zan. Zero surprise on the guy's face but somehow that didn't seem strange. "The world is awful small, isn't she?"

Two

Zan tried to school his expression into a mask of polite professionalism as he took the seat on Deacon's left. It was hard to do though. Gone was the roguish man in leather. He'd been replaced by a proper businessman wearing a suit the color of the ocean depths, jacket slung over a chair to show off the detailed, delicate embroidery on Deacon's vest. Silver thread glinted in the harsh overhead lighting; impossible to miss. As were the leather bracelets on both wrists and the large lapis ring on Deacon's right index finger. Zan swallowed hard, trying not to stare at Deacon's forearms, exposed by the tightly rolled up sleeves of his pristine white shirt. Up close Zan could better see the tattoos dotting Deacon's tawny skin; big, bold florals ending in a line of thorny vines curling around his elbow.

Deacon had looked good in leather. But now, in a three-piece suit and his hair slicked into place, he looked powerful. It made something inside Zan squirm.

Deacon brushed a stray strand of gray hair out of his face and said, "Looks like I'm in the best hands, Rucker." A tiny smirk stole over his face. "I'm sure you have other, more important things to do besides take a new client on a tour. After all, Zan is the best."

Not a question. A statement. A declaration. But almost a dare from this strange, enticing man whom Zan would soon be alone with. The line of sweat trickling down his back wasn't entirely from the overly warm room.

Zan watched as Rucker paused, gaze flicking between he and Deacon as if the older man didn't quite comprehend what Deacon was inferring. Then with a nod, Rucker said, "You bet your ass he is. Zan's the reason we're still chugging along."

You're not wrong there, Zan thought bitterly. He'd done more for Oakside Printing - and Rucker - than anyone else. And he stayed out of some warped sense of loyalty. After all, Rucker had given him a job right out of college, when his prospects had been shit and the interview queues for teaching jobs ruled out anyone who wasn't at the top of their class or a giant kiss-ass. Zan had always been average - average grades, average looks. Sometimes blending into the shadows or skirting the edges of things like crowds wasn't a negative; he'd certainly overheard more little secrets and asides that way, whether he meant to eavesdrop or not. Average looks meant dating wasn't always so fun, and those ridiculous apps pretty much encouraged outright lying. And he hated the idea of filtering himself to death in order to appear taller, thinner, more muscular, more square-jawed.

And then he'd found the job opening at Oakside and he and Rucker had hit it off in the interview. Eighteen years had passed, and Oakside was still a little eclectic, a little eccentric, but Zan actually enjoyed the job. He could proudly say that the business was aloft partially because of his efforts, but it hadn't been his hands alone. Even Rucker, as boisterous and preening as he could be, knew how to make things happen. He was lucky, all things considered. A steady paycheck, a job that didn't follow him home (most of the time), and he wasn't usually called in on his days off for things like a building tour.

He was, however, not at all miffed his day off had been interrupted by someone like Deacon.

Rucker trundled off with a cheery wave and then Zan and Deacon were alone. Deacon was still leaning back in his chair, as casual and relaxed as anything. Then suddenly, he slapped his hands on the armrests and got to his feet. "This makes sense," he said, gaze darting about the dingy conference room.

"What does?" Zan tried not to look startled by Deacon's burst of energy.

"You. This place."

That made him snort. "Gosh, thanks. Me and a crappy conference room go together." Shit. He wasn't supposed to be mouthy with clients. *Prospective* clients, especially not them. Rucker was probably already pacing in his office, eagerly awaiting Zan to return Deacon from their tour so the contracts could be signed and Rucker could have a nice deposit in the company's accounts. He did not need to lose Deacon's business, especially because he couldn't keep his mouth shut.

But Deacon didn't seem bothered at all. "Nah, I mean you struck me as the business orderly type. Very detailed." Deacon's gaze raked over him. Scrutinizing. Assessing. "Smart, too. I knew it."

"You knew it from a single, three minute interaction?"

"I'm pretty good at figuring people out." Deacon smiled. He had a gold tooth, the bottom right canine. Who the hell was this guy? "We know who the real decision maker here is, yeah?"

The warmth in his stare made something tighten in Zan's gut. This guy was trouble and it just so happened Zan had been on the lookout for such a thing. Those stupid apps were so fake, so trite. But Deacon was real - gorgeous, strange, and apparently some kind of business owner. Which he should really figure out what Deacon needed from a mass printer. As in do his job.

"Well, I appreciate that," Zan replied as he opened the door to the conference room. He motioned Deacon forward then lead them down the opposite hall, toward the printing press and binding centers. "So what kind of things will we be printing for you?"

"Some marketing materials. Posters, brochures. Boring shit."

Zan nodded. "What's the non-boring shit?"

That made Deacon light up. With the noise of the printing presses clunking in the background, he said, "I own Rochester Press." With a glint in his eyes, he asked, "Have you heard of it?"

Zan felt faint. *Heard of it?* Rochester was the biggest indie publisher of erotica and surreal fiction. He was a huge fan, had been since their first books were published over half a decade ago. He managed to not gape like a fish before responding. "Straight up? Yeah, yeah I've heard of you. I've got at least four shelves of your books."

Deacon's grin grew wider, cannier. "I'm honored. Though they're not *my* books, yeah? I'm just the spotlight, not the talent on stage." He tapped the side of his head. "I admit some of it's a level of creative juice I just don't have up here. But that's why they're the authors and I'm the guy helping them find their audience."

He liked that explanation. It told him Deacon didn't think too highly of himself and didn't see his business as a way to solely make money. But as an endeavor of love. And Rochester published the strange and ephemeral, the raw and sensual, the kind of writing that felt like the best sex or a shot to the gut. It wasn't for everyone, but most of the books Zan reread every year were from them.

Suddenly the enigma that was Deacon made more sense.

"Well, I want to help you publish more," Zan said, managing to not gush all over Deacon. "Because what you do is needed for readers. To shake things up, to make them question. Make them think."

With a curious tilt to his head, Deacon closed the short distance between them. "Gimmie a minute to be a complete egocentric. But I gotta know..." His smile fell away and Zan mourned its loss. "You got an absolute 'this is the book I have with me on a deserted island and it numbs the pain of the rum being gone' pick from us?"

It was a no-brainer. "*Philosophy of Ivy and Mercy.*" Zan stared hard at Deacon. "I can't even begin to tell you what that book did to me as I was reading. And after I'd finished? People joke about book comas but..." He shook his head, ran his fingers through his hair. He'd rushed to the office after showering away the bike ride and hadn't scrunched the bit of wave in his brown hair with pomade. He could feel some of the frizz gently snag on the platinum ring on his right hand.

Zan hissed and yanked his hand away, but the hair caught on the prongs holding the smoky topaz stone in place. "Ah, ah, here. Let me help." Deacon caught his wrist, his grip gentle. "You stay put. I'll get it."

With Deacon this close, Zan couldn't ignore the little things. The silver buttons on Deacon's vest bore different patterns - flowers, a bee, a fleur de lis. They matched at a distance, but up close, they added a bit of charm to an otherwise rather pressed and proper suit. And the way he smelled set Zan's mouthwatering; something dark and heady, like the tang of ocean air near thick summer vegetation baking in warm soil. He'd never smelled anything like it on another's skin and it made his insides roil.

Deacon was dangerous. It was a very good thing Zan liked a little danger.

Carefully, with warm fingers, Deacon untangled the hair and ring. Zan pulled his hand free at Deacon's nod. "Thanks."

"You bet." Deacon backed up to a polite distance, but his head kept that curious tilt. "Any chance I can get that tour?"

Zan was feeling more than a little flirty, and a little off kilter, from those few seconds of closeness. So he smiled and said, "Of course. And since you saved me just now, I'll even let you try your hand at binding a book if you want."

Deacon looked delighted. "Gonna let an untrained stranger go ham on a big, expensive machine? You're wild, I like it."

If it made Deacon smile like that? Absolutely. "You game?"

"Fuck yes."

Three

Deacon's questions about their operations were considered, thorough. For all the man's strange, enigmatic energy, he clearly knew what he was talking about. As their conversation veered away from bubbly flirtatiousness into printing optics and schedules, Zan relaxed. This was the easy part - he knew every machine down to each nut and bolt, which roller squeaked and which ones they'd just replaced, and the experience in years each staff member had. Rochester was a busy, but still rather small, independent publisher, and Zan had no doubts they could keep up with demand.

"Now, if one of your books hits a bestseller list, we'll have to talk about that," he said with a grin. "But outside of something like that then yeah, we can keep up no problem."

"And if we bring on more stores to stock the titles?"

The careful way Deacon was studying him told Zan this was a serious question, one Deacon had stakes in. He understood that on a lot of levels; staking part of your business on a risk, no matter how mild, was always a bit of a shot in the dark. If he were Deacon, he'd be racked with nerves. "Any head's up you can give is good. Contractually, we need a month."

Deacon mouthed the word *contractually* as if he were testing it out. "But if we can give you more...that's what I'm hearing and not hearing."

Zan had to chuckle at that. "Yeah, any advance notice is helpful."

"Good, good. I'm a hands-on guy, so the notice might come from me."

Zan's gaze absolutely didn't go right to Deacon's tattooed fingers as he pointed at himself. Nope. Not at all. "That's a nice change of pace. A lot of companies we work with have one contact and half the time they don't answer quickly." He frowned. "It can make things tough."

"I bet. Nah, I'm usually first in, last out. Wouldn't have started a company if I wasn't willing to put in the time."

And that Zan could respect. They started to walk again, back to the door that would take them into the office, and Deacon easily fell in step with him. Zan realized the more time he spent with Deacon, the more aware of the *man* he became. Like now - he was noticing Deacon's easy stride, his long legs carrying him with a grace Zan figured came from all the skateboarding he'd done in the past. And since his mouth usually got the best of him, he had to ask. "So, you said you used to skateboard. Was it just a thing to do, or was it more serious?"

They parted so Melly, one of the younger employees, could rattle by with a cart full of freshly printed books. "Last batch out today, Zan," she said, giving him a thumb's up.

"Good, good. The museum will be happy."

"And thank fuck for that," she shot back with a grin.

"Oh, I like her," Deacon said. "Nice to know you're not one of those uptight bosses."

Zan's eyebrows went up. "How do you know that?"

"I can just tell."

Well, he'd take it. Zan steered them back to the conference room, then went to fetch the contract paperwork and two bottles of water. He was only gone for a few minutes but in that time, Deacon had put his jacket back on and cracked open a book he must have pulled from his bag. Zan eyed the bag discerningly; Italian leather, black, classic. A little worn in the way well cared-for leather got over the years. Maybe it was presumptuous to judge a man by any clothing or item on his person, but Zan could appreciate an investment piece. A leather bag, a suit, a trail bike. Something to last, to enjoy over the years, and to subtly make a statement, if you were into that kind of thing. He wasn't sure yet what it said about Deacon, but in his book none of them were bad. It just made him more curious, especially in a world full of waste and fast fashion.

"You never saw this," Deacon said as he put the book aside.

"I do enjoy a secret," Zan replied. He took the seat across from Deacon and began sorting through his folder. "Is that an advanced copy of some kind?" He narrowed his eyes but couldn't make out the cover.

And then Deacon turned it over to show off the plain gray cover. *Yanna Grisolf.* The author of *Philosophy of Ivy and Mercy*. Zan's mouth dropped open. "You're shitting me," he stage whispered. "I thought she retired from writing."

"One more." Deacon pointed at Zan, expression gone serious. "And you don't know that, either."

"One more? Is this her last, then?"

"Yeah. She said she's written all she can and now she wants to do something else."

Zan reeled. Yanna Grisolf was one of the best writers on the fucking planet. News of her retirement had spread far and wide in literati and artist circles. Her readings packed tiny bookstores and rambling cafes, and her signings could go five hours. (Not that Zan had ever stood in line for five hours multiple times for signed copies to gift to friends and family.) And Yanna was a force of nature; nearly eighty, still downhill skiing and parachuting out of planes. A madwoman of the highest order, afraid of nothing.

Another bit of Deacon's puzzle clicked into place. Yanna had a similar vibe to Deacon. It made sense.

"To do what?" He had to know.

Deacon smiled. Delighted once more. "To learn how to race cars."

"Shut the fuck up."

"I know." He leaned back in his chair and put his hands behind his head. The overhead light glinted off his silver buttons and the chains around his neck and Zan could see, between the gap in Deacon's collar, where more ink spread across his skin.

Fuck.

He was a sucker for tattoos on anyone, but on a guy like Deacon, they simply *fit*. As though they belonged on his skin, like he'd been born with them. Zan had dated a woman years ago who had been the same; inked to high heaven but every tattoo was perfectly placed. He'd spent a lot of time mapping all those lines with his fingers and tongue. The desire to do so on Deacon made Zan shift in his chair a little.

Deacon was still talking and Zan realized he'd zoned out because he'd *been staring*. And Deacon apparently didn't notice, so Zan's brain caught up with reality as Deacon was saying, "So yeah, I'm reading it and it's friggin' genius. And since you're a big fan, I think you might actually like this one more than *Philosophy*."

Zan blinked. "What? No way. Impossible."

"Never say never. You do that too much and then the word means nothing anymore."

Zan let that rattle around in his head for a moment, then slid the stack of papers to the middle of the table. "Okay, as badly as I want to keep talking about Yanna's writing with you, I gotta know." He tapped the papers with a finger. "You in?"

Deacon studied his face, then gave a slow nod. "As long as you're the one in charge of our jobs, then yeah. I don't want to be pawned off to someone else. Our authors deserve the best." And he gave Zan the kind of smile that *promised*.

The compliment warmed him, even though Zan realized this was just his job and not some momentous accomplishment. It's not like he was flying to the fucking moon; he just ran a print shop. He swallowed against a dry throat. "Do you want to see some of our previous work?"

"No need." Deacon leaned forward, attention now rapt on Zan. "I scoped you out a while back, but due diligence and all that." He drew a circle in the air, framing Zan's face. "And Rucker might be a character, but I bet he knew putting your face on Oakside's website was the smart money. Everybody loves a face like yours."

Oh god. He was going to ask, wasn't he? *Of course he was.* But Zan's voice was a little rough anyways as he asked, "Like mine how?"

Deacon got to his feet, the roller chair moving backwards a few inches as Deacon strode forward. He came close, closer than Zan expected and yet not close enough according to his overactive, mildly confused libido. "You want a compliment, just ask," Deacon said. He was taller than Zan by a few inches and such a small space had never felt so good. He liked being towered over, being handled a little. And this close (*so close, so deliciously close*), Zan could smell him again. The intent in Deacon's eyes spoke volumes, but he kept his words quiet. "So this one's for free. A face like yours, with those pretty brown eyes and wide cheekbones. Open. Trusting. The stranger at the bar everyone's drawn to, cause they want to see what's behind those glasses."

Deacon gave the bridge of Zan's glasses a tiny tap, barely a brush of his fingertip. It made Zan shiver. "You're not saying that just to get better treatment, right?"

His mouth. His stupid, loud, runaway mouth.

But Deacon only laughed. "Nah. I know Oakside's good. But I saw you this morning and then remembered where I'd seen this face before and realized it must have been Fate or one of her sisters either punking me, or trying to tell me something. Cause you..." He brought his big, tattooed hands up to frame - but not touch - Zan's jaw. "You don't gotta believe in ol' Fate to wonder if we shouldn't take a chance here or there. Been a while since I leapt without looking."

Deacon's mind was a maze, a labyrinth of strange but connected thoughts and feelings and philosophies on existing (and apparently *Ivy and Mercy*). And Zan loved it. He wanted to know more, was greedy for the glittering lines of Deacon's brain. "Do you like canoeing?" Zan asked. He hovered his hands over Deacon's arms for a moment, got a nod, and then got to rub his fingertips and palms over fine fabric. "I go every weekend. I know some great spots, quiet ones."

"Good for a picnic?"

"Absolutely."

"I fucking love it." Deacon's gaze drifted to Zan's mouth, then shot back up. Something shimmered there. Anticipatory. It gave Zan a little thrill to see Deacon's expression shift to something more curious, more heady. "Text me the details. Tell me what to bring and I'll be there."

"Okay."

"Okay."

When Deacon finally left, Zan's number in his phone and a copy of the contract with Oakside in his bag, Zan slumped against the wall by the front door for a moment. His head felt too full but he was grinning. It tugged at his face, that smile, and made something fuzzy and light *pop* in his chest.

When he went back to the conference room to clean up, he saw Deacon's book resting on the table. The note sticking out of the top simply read: "I'll get it back from you. Enjoy but remember...you never saw this."

Four

Zan sat in his car and stared out at the parking lot. It was little more than a square bit of dirt packed down enough so the average family sedan or minivan could get in and out without much trouble. He was the only one here and he was twenty minutes early for his date.

Was date the right word? Neither he nor Deacon had actually said it three days ago. They hadn't said it in any of their...

Zan checked his phone and whistled softly.

About three hundred texts in that same time span.

And yet here he was, waiting on a man who seemed to be hyped for their canoeing slash picnic encounter.

Date

Okay, so it was a date. Only he had no solid assurances that Deacon thought the same way. Maybe he should use his big mouth for his benefit for once.

While Zan was grumbling at himself for not clarifying what this meetup actually was, a mud-splattered utility wagon spun into the lot, back tires kicking on loose dirt and gravel. The car was almost the same color as the dirt, it was so covered. But even through the grime, Zan could see dozens of battered, sun-warped stickers from local bands that played the kind of music that got you an elbow in the face and then an apology from the person who hit you, cause the hit hadn't been on purpose. At least half of those bands weren't together anymore, and it was almost funny to see the progression of stickers show how their careers had changed. This guitarist to this new wave metal band, then the lead singer over to a punk rock group, etc.

The car stopped in a parking spot and a tattooed hand poked out of the open window, giving him a cheeky wave. Through the glass of his passenger window Zan saw Deacon grinning and had to smile back in return. The guy's energy was infectious. Deacon looked dashing even now in lightweight hiking gear and Zan realized that some guys could in fact pull off camo unironically.

They got out of their cars and met up around the back of Zan's as taillights flickered and the hatch on Deacon's car began to open. "I brought my usual kit plus..." He drew out an honest-to-God picnic basket. "Lunch. Made it myself this morning."

This charming man in dark green camo pants held the basket aloft like a prize and Zan shook his head. "Anyone ever tell you you're too much in the fun kind of way?"

"You just did. And I like it." Deacon tipped his head down to peer at Zan over the top of his sunglasses. "Canoeing on a first date is a bold move. Some might say brave, too. Still a lot of mosquitoes this time of year." While Zan was processing that, Deacon slid forward, into Zan's space. "What if I get bit, then start itching just as things get interesting."

Not even in Deacon's presence for three minutes and the man was twisting Zan up inside. He'd managed this morning, while huddled over a mug of coffee, to push aside thoughts of exploring tattooed skin with his lips, then his tongue. That all came roaring back now, strong enough to almost make Zan say fuck it and ask Deacon if he wanted to come back to his place. Instead, what came out was, "So this is a date?"

Zan had tried to go for playful, but Deacon's mouth twisted down into a frown. "Hold up, man. Is this not?" His hand tightened on the picnic basket and panic flooded Zan's system. "Ah, shit. I knew I shouldn't have inferred -"

But Zan was right there, wrapping his hand around Deacon's so they both held the basket. The byproduct of that movement closed the distance between them and left Zan looking up, right into Deacon's eyes as the other man pulled down his sunglasses. "I realized this morning I didn't actually say that it was, which is a bad move on my part." Zan raised an eyebrow, tightened his hand on Deacon's. "Cause it is, but only if you want it to be. No pressure. You're just..." He waved his free hand in the air. "I don't even know. Something special. Different. And I wanted to get to know you better."

The intensity of Deacon's stare nearly knocked Zan back a couple of paces. "Special, you say. Shit, man, I haven't been called that in a long time." And Deacon's grin was something to behold. "I like it."

"Yeah?" Hope was a thing fluttering in Zan's chest but, cynic that he was, he had to keep one foot on the ground, in case it all got swept out from under him. This wouldn't be the first time someone had played a cruel joke.

"Yeah. You've got this vibe. Like, laid-back and everything but under that, there's a fire. I see it." And gods help him, Deacon leaned down, his breath ghosting over Zan's lips. "And I really like fire."

This was happening.

Fuck.

"Can I -"

Under his palm, Deacon's hand tensed but the man himself looked besotted. "You kiss me right now, I'm gonna drop our lunch and then where does that leave us?"

"Shit outta luck?"

"Yeah, sure."

Zan craned his neck, angling. Hoping. "Do you care?"

"Not a fucking bit." Deacon's last word was said against his lips. It was sweet, his kiss; soft and easy, comfortable. Zan could feel the tension drain from his body while Deacon kissed him like he was some precious thing. And he kissed back, eager to feel how Deacon responded (which he did, a quiet groan slipping out while Deacon gripped his shoulder).

It was the kind of thing that made Zan melt, and the care in this little kiss left his head spinning. What grounded him was the slide of Deacon's fingertips against the side of his neck.

Deacon broke off with a final peck to Zan's lips. "That okay?"

He swallowed hard, nodded. "Yeah. It's good."

"You sound a little breathless there, Zan." Deacon's smile made Zan want to dive in again, discover if he could make Deacon gasp. "I've always been told I'm a good kisser."

"Lucky me."

"You bet your ass." Deacon winked. "And I'm real good at that, too."

Zan wanted him to say it but teasing the other man felt far too good to simply let it go. "Asses?"

Deacon backed up and finally their hands parted. Zan felt the loss of warm skin and instantly hated it. But Deacon simply said, "Kissing them. Love it," and watched Zan throw his head back and laugh. This was going to be a hell of an afternoon.

Zan rented a cozy little canoe from the local ranger hut and once they got it into the river, he was more than happy to take up the paddle. "I feel like I'm being courted," Deacon said cheerily as they floated on a small current. "Got my own chauffeur down a pristine waterway. Moss hanging off the trees, sunlight through the leaves." He pointed to the right, where a crane stood in the water near the shore. "Giant ass birds making weird noises. And me sitting on my ass while you do all the work."

Zan gave a little bow, making Deacon laugh. The man had a nice laugh, a nice voice, and now that Zan knew it could rumble and purr like any proper romance story hero, it made the sound even better. "You remind me of some of those heroes in the books you publish. The early ones."

"I miss those," Deacon sighed, leaning back on his elbows against the boat. "I mean, they were filthy if you read between the lines but I thought subtle was the best way to build up our customer base. Like we'd turn readers off if we published straight up smut." He waggled his bushy eyebrows. "I should have known better."

"No kidding. We all act like it's some big secret but people just want porn."

Deacon smirked at him. "Am I talking to a connoisseur? I would *love* to hear about that."

"You are an aggressive flirt." But Zan couldn't stop smiling. Deacon knew when to be professional and when to let loose, and it was clear to him that the other man felt comfortable enough to strip off the veneer of business owner and let Zan see who he really was.

"Ooo, okay, now we're getting into the meat of things. A little aggression and this one gets hot under the collar." Deacon drummed his fingertips on the canoe. "Gotta say I'm curious to explore that, if we keep getting along and you're into it."

Zan refused to flush, or back down. "Think you're up for it?"

Somehow Deacon's lazy sprawl became more suggestive; his thighs parted and his hips canted up a little. "Think you are?"

Jesus Christ, this guy. He knows how hot he is and yet that confidence isn't anything but a turn-on. Zan chose not to answer, giving only the barest hint of a smile. From the way Deacon's eyes widened, he hadn't been expecting that but was delighted nonetheless.

Zan paddled them around a slight bend, bringing their canoe into one of his favorite spots. The sun hit just right here, sending scattered beams of light through lush green leaves overhead, and the thick smell of warm dirt and clear river water became stronger. "Lunch is whenever we feel like it, right?" he asked, holding out a hand to Deacon once he'd tied the boat to a nearby dock.

"Such a gentleman." Deacon let Zan pull him to shore, and then that sneaky son of a bitch let Zan take his weight, twisting them so Deacon was the one to land on his back. Zan crashed into him, palms slapping into the ground, the solidness of Deacon under him cushioning the blow. "Hi there."

"Hi," Zan gasped, purely out of shock rather than any injury. Deacon had made sure Zan would be as safe as could be when an utter madman pulled them to the ground twenty feet from shore. "What was that?"

"I wanted to repay the gentleman." The glint in Deacon's eye made him shiver. "See, I'm *not* a gentleman. I'm a rogue and a scoundrel, like some of the heroes in some books I published years ago. I'm thinking I ought to do reprints of them, so I thought I'd try out a few real-life scenarios. See if they're as romantic as I remember." The touch that brushed Zan's hair out of his eyes was feather-light and yet somehow more intimate than the kiss they'd shared. "Because the gentleman tells me there's a market for refined smut and it turns out I *just* signed a contract with a very talented book printer."

It took him a moment, but Zan was able to catch up with Deacon's merrily cartwheeling mind, following the tangled thought out to its conclusion. "So I'm the gentleman," he said softly, "and currently in the arms of a scoundrel and that scoundrel wants me *oh shit –*" Zan's words snapped to a halt as Deacon slid his hands down, down, *down*. His touch was still gentle and Zan knew if he said stop, Deacon would in a heartbeat. But he really wanted to see if Deacon would go for the full-on ass grab. Cause right now Deacon's palms were flat on the small of Zan's back - like his own palms were flat on the ground, holding him up while Deacon's held him still. And he needed those hands to move about two inches further south. "Fuck, Deacon."

"Is that a no?"

Zan held back a gasp. He was not going to get an erection here, now. But that sweet, almost bitter, feeling rose up in him and he had to bite the inside of his cheek to keep from squirming. "It's a *keep going but be careful.*"

"Mmm. I like it. Restraint even when it would be so easy to give in." Deacon slid those hands down (*finally, thank fuck*) and gently squeezed Zan's ass. "Next you're gonna tell me we'll have a delightful picnic lunch and then on our way back to the canoe, we'll get caught in a rainstorm and have to huddle together for warmth. And there will only be one bed and then we'll finally cave to our desires."

"Who doesn't love a - ah, Deacon my *fucking god* - classic trope?" Deacon's fingers squeezed once more. They were so strong and warm even through Zan's pants and he was really in danger at this point. Because Deacon was right below him, smiling like Zan was the most delightful thing on the planet. Joy and lust battled in him for dominance. "And since the rogue did a gentlemanly thing and made us lunch from scratch, by hand, then I think he protests too much."

Silence stretched, backed by the lapping of waves and the call of a bird overhead. Here, the sunlight dappled them in swatches of gold and Zan felt their warmth keenly, making him more aware of the warm man beneath him. "Yeah, yeah I probably do," Deacon finally replied, voice a little hoarse as he stared up at Zan. "But that's only cause people expect me to be quirky or weird all the time, instead of someone who thinks down a slightly different path on occasion. But you..."

"Hmm?"

Zan met Deacon halfway, knowing whatever they were building would lead to another kiss. Zan got swept up in it this time, lost to its tides. He floated and yet felt *everything* because everything about Deacon was present. Dazzling. And he wanted more.

"I'm already having a fucking *blast*, just so you know."

Zan's laugh rose in the small space now between their lips. "And you say I'm the madman."

Five

Lunch was after a hike up a small, densely treed hill leading to a view Zan had yet to find a rival for.

"Wow." Deacon turned in a slow circle, arms outstretched. "Did you just stumble on this place?"

"Doubt I'm the first, even with the way it's hidden off the paths." Zan sat on the ground to poke through the open basket. "But between the view, the company, and...is this brie?"

Deacon smiled.

Zan could only praise the food Deacon had so thoughtfully packed, from the delicate, tiny circles of brie to cucumber sandwiches to containers of fruit. "I would have brought my famous stew, even tried to think of a way to make it travel. But I guess you'll have to experience that another time." Deacon ambled over, hands in his pockets, scarf whipping in the slight wind. He really was pretty in a rough-tumbled, salt breeze kind of way. And knowing what Zan did about how the man wore a three piece suit, it only added to the appeal. There was no sanding down Deacon's jagged edges, but they were refined by experience and age. Though Zan knew they weren't terribly far apart, less than a decade, something about Deacon made him timeless. He envied the man's stance, the way he held himself.

"Another time?"

Deacon shrugged, the movement effortless, easy. "I mean, I'm having a fucking blast." He flopped down beside Zan as if the ground would simply give, jelly-like, against his body. Zan would have never, could have never, done the same. "So I figure if you're amenable, we do this again. We can keep the birds and the sunshine but maybe you come to my place." He wiggled closer to Zan, eyes glittering. "Maybe I make you dinner, we tear through some wine, and then I do this..."

Zan felt that pull once more, magnetic and almost hair-raising, to Deacon as the man leaned in. "You do what?" Zan teased.

Deacon's mouth hovered above his own, that lanky frame boxing him in. "Whatever you want, hot stuff. I'm a pleaser."

"You realize that you're making a lot of promises."

"Not promises." Deacon brushed his lips over Zan's. "Guarantees. Money-back."

Despite the delicious tension in the air, Zan couldn't help but chuckle. "We better eat."

Deacon's pout was miniscule but unmistakable, but it didn't stop him from thumbing at Zan's bottom lip. "One more?"

As if Zan could resist.

***

"Might sound exaggerated, but this is legit the best date I've ever been on."

Zan turned his head to the right to look at Deacon. "Funny. I was thinking the same thing."

It was almost a whimsical thing, existing beside someone else and looking up at a bright blue autumn sky. Something about the moment *clicked*. And looking at Deacon now, slightly rumpled and creased but still bright with energy and life, left Zan feeling content.

Deacon broke the silence by pointing up and saying, "Bunny or lizard?"

Zan considered the squashed bit of cloud above them. "Werebunny. See the fangs?" Zan also pointed up at the cloud, where a wispy bit of white curved off what he thought was the bunny's mouth.

"Ah, but do werebunnies have big, long tails like that? I mean, look at that fucker. It's like a dragon tail."

"Okay then it's some kind of weird hybrid."

"Got it. Though..." Deacon broke out laughing. "It reminds me of when you get those fucking weird dogs, where one parent was a big dog and the other some itty-bitty yappy thing. And like the dog has a wiener body but a bulldog head or some shit. So this poor bunny..." He laughed again, the sound buoyant, joyful. Zan began to laugh too; the image was too ridiculous. "The poor bunny gets railed by a dragon and we get werebunny dragon lizard thing?"

"Ooof, that's every tabletop RPG player's nightmare."

As unexpected as a sun flare, Deacon's face lit up. "Wait, wait. Okay, we gotta seriously talk if you're into that sort of thing."

Zan immediately thought to the jars of dice and thick, hardback books stored away in the office closet. The room was little more than a spot for his gaming computer, desk, and a floor lamp, and the closet was tiny. But he'd never had the heart to get rid of or donate his tabletop gaming gear. Those games had saved his sanity as a teenager, when hormones running rampant left him feeling adrift and unlike any of his peers. The local comic shop became a safe haven, and those rulebooks and jars of dice holy relics. And every now and then he'd open the closet and look upon those happy bits of his youth, remembering late night sessions where heroes pulled dusty bags of gold and strange magical objects from the hands of crumbling skeletons and out of spider-infested pits.

"It's been a long time," he admitted, "but I have all the stuff still. I'm sure it's ages out of date-"

"Nah, the old stuff is the *best*," Deacon gushed, now turned on his side to study Zan fully. The intensity in his eyes might have made Zan wilt years ago, but over forty him found comfort in it. Deacon was perhaps someone who understood, who got what it was like to dive headlong into something new and love every moment, let it consume those minutes where otherwise the mind would run pell-mell. Reading, biking, canoeing all quieted the worries; and bringing back his love of tabletop games could be another outlet. "I've got every edition of Dungeon Delve, except the newest because they fucked with the rules and it just...defeats the whole point of the game, which is to have big-ass swords and fight evil and be epic."

Deacon's obvious passion rang in his ears and made Zan's heart pound hard. He liked Deacon, really liked him, and it had been so damn long. "You know what?" Zan said, also turning on his side. "I think I should dig all those books out and just do a full nerd session, relearn everything. And then we should play Dungeon Delve."

"It's like riding a bike, man. You get that character sheet in front of you and it just...comes back. Bam! Like a mallet to the face, but in a fun way." Deacon frowned. "You know what I mean."

Zan did. "Okay, let's see how we mesh on this. Favorite starting class? Mine's dominion mage, cause they get spells and damage with their staffs."

"I like it. Smart and ferocious. But yeah, me...thief. Always."

He snorted. "Somehow that makes sense."

Deacon propped up his left leg and ran his hand up it until his palm rested on his knee. "I figured your memory was sharp enough to recall how good I look in leather."

"Fishing for compliments?" Zan nudged closer, until their shoulders touched. "All you have to do is ask. Though I think you know how fucking good looking you are, Deacon."

That forced a chuckle out of Deacon. "I think what I get mostly is 'Whoa, dude must have had a hard life. Look how grizzled he is.'"

"Not grizzled." Now Zan snuggled into Deacon's side, put his palm on a firm chest. "If they're saying that, they have no taste and then they don't matter. Cause you're hot as hell. Like this or in that fucking suit you had on or in leather pants and a red shirt, sitting on top of a concrete ramp like some kind of skatepark pirate king."

Callused fingers tipped Zan's chin up. "I always did like pirates. Something about their middle finger to the rules."

"Says the man who publishes alien barbarian romances."

"Hey, those are bestsellers at Rochester for a reason. People are more weird than they give themselves credit for, yeah?"

Zan closed the distance between them. He needed Deacon's lips on his, right now. His blood felt like it was on fire and the need pooling in his stomach made goosebumps pop up on his skin. Deacon wasn't like anyone else, and Zan hoped he'd get the chance to unravel the fascinating ways he saw the world.

"Someone's eager," Deacon whispered as he ran his hand down Zan's side, the touch ending in a firm grip on Zan's right hip. "We've got a long trek back before anything else can happen."

Zan smirked. "Not an outdoor sex kind of guy?"

"Bum hip aside, fucking in the grass just never had any appeal." Deacon gave an exaggerated shudder. "You don't know who is watching. Could be a deer, which okay Bambi, get down with your bad self." He dropped his voice, expression gone very serious. "Or you could be just doing your thing, woo all's fun and shit and then there's a *fucking bear*. And I like my intimate encounters to be without the chance of being shoved down a bear gullet."

Laughing, Zan shoved to his feet and offered Deacon a hand up, which the other man accepted. "No crashing into me this time?" he teased.

"Nah, I gotta come up with another move worthy of a scoundrel, since I've now sullied my reputation by being afraid of getting devoured by a bear while fucking outside."

"You wild man. An utter cad still."

Deacon ran a hand through his hair, his smile pleased. "Yeah?"

"Remember...best date ever. And apparently I have a thing for scoundrels."

"Oh yeah. Then shall the scoundrel paddle us back when we get to the river?"

Zan edged in close enough so he could run his fingertips over the stubble on Deacon's cheek. "I would love that."

Six

The rain started when they were halfway to the river. Though calling it "rain" was a misnomer. It had begun as a few errant drops; not surprising for the volatile autumn weather in this part of the country, so close to the coast and so far north. They both had waterproof, hooded jackets that could handle a bit of rain.

What none of their gear could handle was a downpour and one that was chased with lightning and thunder.

Zan managed to find a copse of trees thick enough to block the worst of it, but the lightning worried him. Over the deafening rain, he yelled to Deacon, "There's a ranger hut up the next hill but that exposes us more to the lightning." Zan pulled out his phone and shielded it with his other arm while he scrolled through the notes app. "Hold on, I know it's here..."

"What the hell are you doing?" Deacon yelled back. "We're about to be crispy critters. Shouldn't we just get down the river? Maybe it's better back the way we came, yeah?"

"Ah!" Zan turned his phone to Deacon. "Found it!"

"The fuck is that?"

Zan grinned, despite the water dripping off the end of his nose and the chill seeping into his fingers, making them cramp. "Coordinates for an old house I hiked by a while back."

Deacon stared at him, then laughed; the sound short and sharp. "Holy shit, you actually noted that."

"Just in case!" Zan patted his waterproof backpack, trying not to be too smug. "Cause you never fucking know and I'm not about to be a —"

"Crispy critter?"

"Yeah, exactly."

With the coordinates set into his phone, Zan started to guide them west, toward the house. It was roughly the same distance from the river as their picnic spot, but down in a valley instead of high up. No need to take risks. Deacon was doing a good job of not looking concerned, but the man had thick, pierced salt-and-pepper eyebrows that were currently turned downward, which pinched the outer corners of his eyes. Zan could also see him shivering in his coat and he so badly wanted to pull Deacon close. "Hey, we're almost there," he said after several long minutes, making sure to keep his eyes glued to the GPS. The rain had slowed but the clouds overhead were ominously dark. If the weather front was only just moving in, they might be stuck for a while. The water and snacks he'd packed for their river trip back would hold them through the night, if needed.

But there was something oddly romantic about being stuck in an old house, waiting out a storm.

So to distract from their circumstances, Zan said, "So how would this scoundrel go about tonight, if we are actually stuck in an abandoned house during all this shit?"

After a long moment, Deacon shook his head with a little laugh and swiped at his face. Rain drops glistened as they clung to his cheeks and nose ring. "Well, the scoundrel would count this as the god of romance granting him both the permission and courage to push forward. But the scoundrel would know it would be all on him to court the gentleman properly, to make it up to him since the scoundrel had failed to finish the date like it had started."

Zan could clearly see the story in his head, as if it had been ripped from the pages of one those early tawdry romances Rochester Press had put out. He had a few of them on the shelves, though he hadn't read them in some time. "And I'm guessing what the scoundrel doesn't know is that the gentleman is secretly pleased things turned out this way. Because plans are boring and he likes throwing them in the bin and saying fuck it, let's be scoundrels together."

That got Deacon's attention, despite the roiling of clouds overhead and the distant crack of thunder. It made his eyes light up in a different way, one that promised darkness and secrets and warm breath on skin. As Zan navigated them around a massive dead tree, his hand on Deacon's back, the other man turned to whisper, "Then let's see where the night takes us, yeah?"

"Yeah." Zan swallowed hard. "Sounds good." He quickly did a mental inventory of his pack, eternally grateful to his naive, hopeful, romantic heart that he'd packed condoms and lube. He'd almost left them at home; lingering in the foyer, hand on the zippered pocket of his backpack, wondering if he was being foolish. Apparently not.

"So this abandoned shack -"

"House," Zan corrected. "And it was a little ranger station kind of place, and then after the forestry service built a new station, it looked like someone bought it, fixed it up, then let it go again. It's at the very least a roof over our heads until the storm passes."

"True, true." Deacon seemed to mull that info over as they hiked around a small bend. Zan stopped in his tracks so he could point toward the shack's outline. "Guess we won't know till we get there."

"Won't know what?"

Deacon shot him a smirk. "If it's more than just a roof and four walls."

"That's definitely more than I was expecting."

"Yeah. Agreed." Deacon peered into the windows, craning his neck to see above the line of humidity that had built up on the glass. "Shit, there's a wood stove and a bed, some chairs. We'll be in good shape."

"And...it's locked." Zan jiggled the handle again before reaching above the door frame, fingers blindly feeling for a key. "Come on, come on." Thunder cracked overhead and a fresh burst of rain pummeled them, borne aloft by a biting cold wind.

Deacon stepped back to survey the window. "Do I put an elbow through it?"

"Maybe. In a minute. We'll have to leave a note or something if that happens." Zan stretched, his fingers catching on something small and metal.

Deacon sounded almost ponderous as he replied, "Can't tell if this is a romance scene or a horror novel. *Escape from the Cabin* or some shit like that."

"Ah!" Zan practically ripped the key out of its nook and held it up in triumph. "Let's get the fuck out of this rain."

The lock was old and rusty and it took a frustrating moment to crank it open, but the second the door swung inward, Deacon hauled them inside and slammed the door shut. They were both breathing hard and drenched and freezing and Zan realized how the scene looked. He was standing in the middle of the small room, rain dripping from every part of him, his hair plastered to his forehead. He was probably a little wild eyed and he had the key tight between his numb fingers.

And there was Deacon. Back pressed against the door, palms flat on the wood. Shivering hard. Glittering with raindrops from his eyebrows to his boots. Eyes dark and hot on Zan. The world had narrowed in some intense, almost dangerous way to just the two of them. Trapped in a storm, huddled in a tiny, cobweb-dusted cabin for shelter. Adrenaline surging through their bodies.

"You know, this is the part where the scoundrel might take advantage," Deacon said, pushing away from the door. He prowled toward Zan, sending a shivery, delightful thrill down his spine. Zan wanted it - he wanted to be pounced on, pinned. Taken. Fuck the rain and their wet clothes and the weird, wonderful afternoon they'd had. Right now was all that mattered.

Zan's throat was dry as he replied, "And a good scoundrel asks permission."

Deacon closed in on him, walking them back until Zan bumped into a small table. "I would never, ever not ask," he said softly as he reached up to push Zan's hood down before shoving his own away. Deacon traced Zan's jaw with cold fingers before continuing. "You're shivering. And scoundrel I might be, but I'd never let such a pretty thing freeze. Against my nature."

But Zan wanted, so badly he was practically standing on tiptoe in hopes of meeting Deacon's lips with his own. "Scoundrels shouldn't let 'pretty things' go without being kissed. Especially since this pretty thing found the key that got us inside."

"Sounds like the kind of thing a secret romantic claiming to be a scoundrel would say."

"Does it now?"

Gone was the sense of wonder, the gentle slide of lips. There was hunger in Deacon's kiss this time and even shivering with cold and rain, Zan could feel its heat. Someone groaned as their tongues met and Zan bunched Deacon's soaked raincoat in his fists. That desperation he'd been holding back roared to life, made him pull Deacon's bottom lip between his teeth.

Deacon was a fascinating enigma, a man whose mind reeled and whirled and came to incredible conclusions. He was fun and funny, caring and smart. And hot as hell.

Deacon was also passionate and commanding. Something Zan was learning as the man pushed him backwards. Back and back until Zan hit the wall and Deacon was tearing at the zippers and buttons on his gear. "Supposed to be good against the cold," Deacon muttered as he peeled Zan's raincoat away.

"What?" Zan's head spun with what little blood was left there. Most of it has instantly gone south. He couldn't tell if he was wet from the rain or sweating from nerves and excitement. It didn't matter, because Deacon dropped his own wet outer gear to the floor before pinning Zan with a dark stare. "Deacon?"

"Skin to skin contact. The only real way to warm up." Deacon's gaze slid over Zan, a gauntleted punch wrapped in velvet and about as subtle. "You game?"

Seven

"Fuck yes."

Deacon was on him again, pressed so close Zan could feel they were breathing in tandem. "I do like it when gentlemen give in to me. Makes me feel like I'm earning it."

Zan swallowed hard, biting down on a groan when Deacon kissed the hinge of his jaw. "Earning what?"

"All of it." Deacon pulled back with a steady, almost somber expression on his face. That look took the air out of the room, stole it from Zan's lungs. Made him fixate on dark eyes and heavy brows and the way Deacon gripped at him. "Getting to do this. Drives me crazy, man. I'm not one for dumping my feelings all over the place but you get under my skin and I like it. It's wild." He brushed his fingertips over Zan's cheek. "Really jazzed to see where this goes. It's like an adventure. I almost forgot what that was."

When Zan kissed Deacon again, the other man melted against him. As if he'd been holding back, steadying himself to play the part of the rogue and scoundrel. The seducer, the clever wit, the enigma that made people flock to him. Zan felt all of that *give*, as if Deacon was realizing what he needed and was trusting Zan with that special, secret knowledge. It made Zan want to peel back the layers and see what was underneath. To admire it and hold it close.

Deacon's tongue played with his while strong hands held onto Zan's waist. A lifeline, a tether for them both. And when Deacon skimmed his fingertips over the soft, vulnerable spot just below Zan's ribs, Zan couldn't help but sigh. "That feels good."

"Yeah? Told you." Now Deacon smirked at him, all cunning. "Skin to skin contact. I don't even know if we can get that stove going but we've at least got this." His hands slid higher and Zan let his head rest against the wall, content to have Deacon explore in his own time. "Think that bed is safe enough?"

"Let's find out."

Zan dragged Deacon a few feet to the bed and together they threw back the slightly ratty but warm quilt. The blue fitted sheet was faded with age, but no bugs scurried out and no dust rose when Deacon patted the mattress. "Seems safe enough." He ducked down to look under the bed. "No boogeymen, either."

"Whew, good to know," Zan said with a laugh. The sound echoed in the mostly empty space as lightning cracked across the thick line of dark clouds outside the window. He'd been so caught up in Deacon (and how could he not be?), that he'd all but forgotten the storm and the rain, the darkness blanketing them. "Now come here."

The next few moments were a soft blur of hands and mouths and breathing strained with need. Zan's shirt landed next to Deacon's and that was when his entire vision narrowed in on more thick black ink and piercings. "Goddammit." The rose gold bars through Deacon's nipples glinted in the dark and the man gave an entire body shudder when Zan plucked at one of them. "Fuck, I love these."

"Custom made," Deacon panted out while Zan licked a path down his neck. Deacon wasn't holding back anymore either; he had a firm grip on Zan's ass, kneading the flesh and making Zan rut against him. "I like how pink it is."

When Zan set his lips to Deacon's right nipple and gently sucked, Deacon nearly *growled*. The sound battled with the thunder outside and set Zan's hair on edge. "I like how it looks," Zan shot back. "Especially cause you make it look so damn good. And all this ink?" He trailed his touch down, across Deacon's ribs, to where the tattooed scales disappeared into Deacon's briefs. "Like you were just born with it. It looks right on you."

Something flickered over Deacon's face - an emotion Zan couldn't parse, he didn't know the man well enough yet. But he didn't think it was a bad thing because then Deacon was taking them down to the bed, gentle but firm in his silent command.

Zan yielded. He wanted to. He *ached* with it.

"Kinda wondered what this would be like," Deacon muttered against Zan's chest, mimicking the way Zan had kissed and licked across his skin moments earlier.

Deacon's stubble scraped, his tongue soothed, and his lips explored while his hands worked on the rest of Zan's clothes. "What would what be like?" he managed to get out as Deacon practically tore his pants away. Zan barely had time to lift his hips to assist when Deacon let out another growl and yanked the wet material down to his knees.

"This. You're like that stranger the hero in a movie meets and becomes wicked interested in." Deacon let his fingers dance over Zan's thighs, ignoring the very obvious erection tenting Zan's boxers. "We met and it was like *bam*! I gotta know more. And then I remembered where I saw your face and thought it was some kind of weird Fate thing cause I knew we'd meet again just a few hours later."

"And you didn't have to go all stalker to do so."

Deacon put a hand on his chest dramatically, but his grin told Zan he was in on the joke. "I'd be a shit stalker. I've got that bum hip, remember? Trip over my own damn feet all the time." Zan snorted. "Hand on a holy book or a pirate flag, I swear."

"Or a yellow lily?"

"Or one of those."

Deacon slid up Zan's body with liquid ease; a slinky grace that belied the power in sinewy, lean muscles. Bum hip or not. It was sexy as all fuck and Zan was left groaning into Deacon's shoulder when his heat, his scent cascaded over him.

"Bum hip only acts up during shit like dancing," Deacon whispered in his ear. "Works just fine for fucking. If you're amenable. Cause I'm good with whatever."

Zan gaped at him. "A switch? In the wild? Color me shocked."

Deacon's kiss was brief but hard, his tongue all but invading Zan's mouth with focus and purpose. He nipped at Zan's lower lip, then hooked a thumb at his pack. "Whatever you're good with, hot stuff. I've got supplies in my pack."

"So do I."

"Yeah, but is yours in a specially labeled, waterproof little case?" When Zan just stared, Deacon laughed. "I hate fumbling in the dark for that shit. Then it's all awkward and the lube gets lost in the sheets and you send little condom packets flying. Hell no, man." He shimmied against Zan, pressing their hips and cocks and thighs together and pulling another moan out of them both. "Shit, should have thought about that before I -"

"Deacon."

"Yeah."

"Just fuck me."

Deacon winked, then thrust down. "What, no romance? I thought I was trying to be less scoundrely."

Zan's smack at his shoulder was little more than a pat. "Yeah well, the gentleman would like to be...what did they call it back then? Buggering? Buggered. Fucked. Whatever. Get your cock in me."

Deacon's laugh wasn't even cut off by Zan gripping his ass and squeezing for all he was worth. "Yeah, yeah, okay. A little patience -"

"Deacon, I swear to everything..."

"I got you." Deacon began softly kissing Zan's neck, caressing his sides, and fuck this guy for finding Zan's weak spots with laser-perfect precision. Zan was instantly putty on the mattress. "I got you. Gonna be so good, I promise. And when we're in a proper bed, I'll pull out all the stops." He nipped at Zan's collarbone then moved down, swirling his tongue over a nipple. Zan felt like he'd been struck by the lightning slowly fading outside. "Fuck, Zan. Gorgeous thing."

Zan could only whimper and hold on as Deacon ran his lips and tongue and teeth over his skin. He was a writhing, panting, sweating mess, could feel his cock harden even more. He wanted Deacon to take him apart at the seams and then listen to the rain lull them to sleep. Deacon clearly wanted the same thing, the way he snaked down Zan's body and left nothing untouched. Had it not been for the hot flash of desire arcing through him, Zan felt as though he could have floated away, tended to by this handsome, strange man.

And then Deacon began kissing his inner thighs.

"Fuck. *Fuck*." Zan barely stuttered out the word, trusting the grip he had on Deacon's gorgeous hair was enough to send the message.

"Yeah?" Deacon's eyes were wide and dark and he looked utterly besotted. It made Zan's heart skip.

"Deacon. *Please*."

"Very gentlemanly." Deacon grinned. "And remember, I am *not* a gentleman."

The grip Deacon had on Zan's hips turned almost too tight. It shorted out something in Zan's brain to be held, pinned like that, but even that thought left him when Deacon began mouthing at his cock through his boxers.

He slapped a hand over his mouth to stifle his yelp, but Deacon shook his head. "No one's gonna hear you. Let it out." Deacon suckled the tip, making Zan squirm. "I like a loud lover. Gotta know I'm doing the right thing."

Zan heard the need under Deacon's words - the need to be praised, to know he was doing good, *being good*. So many layers on the man and yet the vulnerable underbelly showed up rather quickly.

Well, he could make it all so *good* for Deacon, too.

Pulse high in his throat, Zan dove to the side of the bed. Deacon trailed after him, half-laughing, half-groaning at their separation. "Which pocket?" he asked, urgency making his skin feel too tight, too hot.

"Left side. Zippered." Deacon was all in now, pressed tightly up against Zan and tangling their legs together. "Could just fuck your thighs, make a mess of you."

Zan nearly choked on his own tongue. "Fucking *fucker*." In the humid darkness, his fingers caught on zipper teeth and he pulled hard. Deacon thrust against him, slid his fingers underneath Zan's boxers. Seeking, teasing, his touch light as he found the sensitive spot between thigh and hip. Zan nearly bucked himself straight off the bed. "Goddammit!"

"Easy there." Deacon's voice rumbled against him. Somehow in Zan's ear and yet plucking strings deep inside him; ones Zan didn't know existed. "Take your time. Still raining a gale out there and it's not like we're gonna be disturbed." The lips on his neck melted Zan into putty once more. Fingers idly stroked Zan's skin. With every touch, he felt both anchored and yet as light as a balloon. It was as if his own body was twisting itself up from the inside, trying to get to Deacon and chase his own pleasure at the same time.

Zan cried in triumph when the zipper finally gave. Ten seconds had felt like ten minutes. Then he was flinging the case onto the bed.

Deacon squinted at him in the dark. Assessing. "Still good?"

"Fucking *please*."

Deacon seemed rather chuffed about the whiny note in Zan's voice. "Good." And when Deacon had them both naked and panting, staring hard at each other, his smile grew. "That is the biggest cock I've ever seen."

Zan huffed but wasn't about to squirm under Deacon's gaze. His attention was firmly rooted on the glint of gold in firm, turgid flesh. "You already felt it."

"Barely." Deacon licked his lips. The ghost of that touch haunted Zan once again. His hips twitched of their own accord. Polite as could be, Deacon handed Zan the condom packet before throwing his arms wide. "Ever been with a guy with a pierced cock? I gotta ask, the way you're staring. Don't want you to scamper off all bunny-like into the underbrush."

Zan kept staring. He wanted it all. Every inch, every ounce, every taste of skin-salt tang, every brush of hair against his cheek or arm or chest. He wanted those piercings dug deep inside him, pulling him from the inside out and making him howl his pleasure to whomever would listen. "Jesus fuck, Deacon."

"And to answer your next question, we're all good. I even put my recent test results in my bag, in case you wanted to double check."

Zan swallowed hard. It *had* been a while since he'd been with anyone, too busy with work to think about much else. "Shit, I didn't even think to do that."

Deacon only smiled at him, the expression gentle. "Why would you? Just tell me straight - you good?"

"Yeah." Zan did the math. "Been about six months since I've been with anyone, and I got tested afterwards. Nothing since."

Deacon lunged for him, hands and mouth hot on Zan's skin. "Then we're good," he whispered against Zan's jaw.

It had felt like they'd been building up to this forever, but it was worth it. The storm, the rain, the shitty abandoned cabin in the woods. The long hike up the hill, the canoe trip. That spectacular lunch and the long moments they spent lying in the grass, staring up at the sky and making jokes about the clouds.

Worth it.

Fumbling with condoms and lube was never sexy but Zan felt especially out of his element when faced with the piercings along the underside of Deacon's cock. "We go careful, so the condom doesn't break." Deacon's words were soft, as if he was afraid of scaring Zan away. *No fucking chance.* "And then you need some attention."

He smirked, liking the way Deacon's eyes widened a little. "You want to touch or watch?"

"Woo boy, you don't mess around." Deacon rolled them until he was starfished under Zan, the both of them laughing at how tangled they'd gotten in the sheets. "What I want is to watch and just when I know your fingers are hitting that spot..." He pulled Zan's right hand to his lips. Zan dragged his fingertips down, catching them on Deacon's damp bottom lip, liking how the other man shuddered at such a simple touch. "I'm gonna pull you into my lap and watch you sit on my cock. Gotta go slow though."

"Again?" Zan failed hard in keeping the lusty frustration out of his voice. "You're gonna fucking kill me, Deacon. Slow isn't for now. We're both naked and ready."

"Yeah but here's the thing, hot stuff. A pierced cock is like nothing else." He nipped at Zan's fingers, chasing them playfully with clicking teeth while grabbing Zan's ass with his other hand. *Those* fingers skated over one cheek; daring, darting close to where Zan needed them. "It's a totally different feeling and these little gems catch just right inside. It feels so goddamn good. I almost passed out the first time I rode pierced dick."

Scratch his objections, then. His blood felt like it was on fire already and Deacon's smoky voice and talk of dicks and piercings and riding until he passed out wasn't helping anything. "Have it your way," he teased.

"Oh. I like the sound of that."

"Yeah?"

"Mmmm, yeah. C'mere."

Deacon dragged out this kiss with slow, deadly precision, leaving Zan to brace one hand on Deacon's chest while he reached behind himself. Deacon's other hand was still there, his touch teasing up and down, round and round. Skating ever so close and then dipping away to caress another spot. "You gotta watch, remember?"

Deacon's pretty eyes popped open and for the first time since they'd started this weird, wonderful date, Zan saw something in Deacon *snap*. The air seemed to spark and shimmer between them. In the space between their lips and the tiny alleys between their fingers where Zan had linked them together. He pulled Deacon up by the neck, biting into their kiss while he touched himself.

Someone groaned. Zan focused on the way Deacon's eyes widened and his breathing hitched before sliding his finger deeper. His cock lay against Deacon's stomach and all that warm flesh felt so good. He'd fingered himself open many times but usually when on his own. He liked it when partners wanted to touch him like that before *taking him*. He'd never had anyone willing to watch, and do so with hot intent.

Never mind the fact that their hands were joined and Deacon's index finger was brushing his hole while Zan pressed inside his body. Deacon seemed to realize it at the same time, because he asked in a husky voice, "Can I?"

Zan moaned and clenched down on his own finger. "Fuck, I wish you would."

"Two hands are better than one."

He groaned and pressed his head into Deacon's shoulder while the other man shook with silent laughter. "Fucker."

Deacon's finger pressed into him and Zan saw white. He arched into it, the feeling what he assumed would be akin to tumbling into an electric fence. He must have made some kind of noise because Deacon's lips were suddenly on his ear and that voice was rumbling through him, shoving a litany of filth into his brain. "Gorgeous thing. Fuck. Zan, oh baby, c'mon. Just a little bit more, open up for me darling. Lemme feel that heat. Cause when you're riding me..." Deacon crooked his finger a little more, sliding it against Zan's. His hips swiveled down, pressing his leaking cock into Deacon's stomach and getting a growl in return. His entire being was lit up, focused solely on chasing pleasure.

"When you're riding me, we're both gonna lose it quick. So no hiding, Zan. Let it out. Let me hear you." Another finger nudged against Zan's hole, making his mouth drop open. "Let me feel it. All of it. I want you to ride me so I can watch for that moment and know you're about to come on me."

Zan choked out Deacon's name as he slid backwards, practically slapping Deacon's hand away. Deacon looked like he might protest, something about Zan not being ready, but he shut up the moment their gazes caught. "Please," Zan whispered.

The slide of Deacon's cock against his sticky skin already had him breathing faster, but the gentle way Deacon helped guide him down made his hair stand on end. There was care in every touch, even if Deacon's words were complete filth. They didn't speak while getting Zan into place, but they didn't need to. There was something like *trust* between them, and the little jolts of awareness that spiked through Zan made it even better.

He remembered to breathe, to relax, even with his heartbeat in his ears. Deacon's cock was thick and short, so the tip nudging inside him quickly turned into *more*. "Easy, easy," Deacon soothed, petting Zan's sides and thighs. He only noticed he was trembling when Deacon touched him, but another wave was set off as the first piercing caught against his hole. "There it is. Just open...good, good. Open for me, Zan." Zan's thighs parted as Deacon's legs drew up behind him; a support for him to brace on. "Goddamn, you are so *warm*."

All Zan could manage was an undignified, "Hng," and another shiver. Eloquence (and time and space) apparently meant nothing when you took your first pierced cock.

Zan liked to say he had a bit of an addictive personality. He'd find something interesting and follow it down a rabbit hole. It was like having a mind full of useless but also fascinating trivia; bits of history, weird science, strange people.

But sex wasn't in that list of fascinations. It was fun, it was sweaty, and ultimately a really good way to blow off steam. But now? He could see *pierced cock* being a problem for the very near future. Those little balls of metal, even protected by the condom, were a revelation. And when Zan bottomed out, all he could feel was warmth and weight and those damanable things rubbing up inside him. "Oh my god. Holy fuck."

Deacon looked rather pleased with himself, despite the glassiness to his eyes. "It's good, yeah? Like we forget how many nerve endings exist until something drags against them." And to illustrate his point, Deacon thrust up a tiny bit. Zan fell on top of him with a groan. "I'll fucking wear my hip down to nothing to make sure you keep making those noises, gorgeous."

"Shut up and fuck me."

"That a request or a demand?" Deacon's gold tooth glinted as he smiled.

Zan hauled himself up, braced his hands on Deacon's chest, and wiggled further down. "Both."

"Perfect."

It took a moment to find the right rhythm but once they did, Zan latched onto it like a man possessed. All the hiking and walking and biking he did had left him with quite a bit of strength in his legs, and in some perverse way, he always got a kick out of watching his own muscles jump when on top of a partner. The slide of sweat-slick skin, the sheer wonder in how bodies fit together, all of it was fascinating and...honestly, quite a bit of a turn-on.

But now he used that strength and flexibility to take Deacon fully, wholly. To make the other man grunt and gasp and whisper dirty little encouragements into the humid air while lightning cracked outside. Dimly, through a lust-soaked brain, he also realized that Deacon never stopped touching him while Zan drove them both to the brink. It was sweet and sexy and he wanted to reward Deacon. "Come here," and he pulled Deacon up by the neck again, getting a soft groan in return as their mouths met. It was messy but real, like good sex should be.

"You are...gonna finish me off," Deacon gasped against Zan's mouth. "It's too soon."

"There'll be later." He looked right into Deacon's eyes as he said it. They might have been just words, but Zan meant it. "But I'm right there, too."

"Thank fuck for that."

Zan stifled a helpless little laugh against Deacon's mouth. The hand suddenly on his cock didn't surprise him (not with that look of intense concentration flashing across Deacon's face) but it sure as hell did make him shudder. The palm stroking him was the right amount of callused and some tiny part of Zan wanted to know what Deacon did to earn them.

"Come on, babe." Deacon was being encouraging but Zan could hear the strain in his voice. He swiped his thumb over the head of Zan's cock and Zan gave a helpless little shiver. "So pretty like this, sitting on my cock like you were made for it."

Zan whimpered. Blinked down at Deacon, who stared back and bit his lip, only to then reach up and tweak Zan's right nipple. The flash of pain-pleasure shot through him and he was gone. Later, he'd realize he'd never orgasmed from a nipple tweak before but he wouldn't be surprised it was Deacon to pull such a reaction from his body. *From him.*

Zan's eyes slammed shut and he toppled forward, only to be caught in strong arms. Deacon whispered mindlessly into his ear and clutched at him and Zan instantly knew he liked the way Deacon groaned when he came.

Eight

The trip back took a lot longer than it should have. It started when Zan had been pressed so tightly into Deacon's side that when he woke up, the indent of a nipple ring stared back at him from his bicep. It had made them both laugh as weak sunlight poured into the cabin and kept them laughing even as Deacon kissed a hot, wet path along Zan's chest.

"No more sex in shitty cabins," Zan begged as Deacon scraped his teeth along Zan's ribs.

"Promise." Deacon held up a finger. "Pinky swear."

They pinky swore and then Zan kissed Deacon hard, with tongue and a bit of teeth.

Even as they trekked back to the canoe, they couldn't keep from brushing up against each other. Deacon was the more tactile of them but Zan found himself leaning into every slide of fingertips or peck on the cheek. It was the kind of thing he might have rolled his eyes at if watching another couple do it, but now he understood. It was *nice* to be wanted, even if that want wasn't always sexual.

And that same want had him now rethinking his past relationships. He wondered if Deacon would be good for a few dates, or if something deeper would flourish. He used to consider himself too old to daydream about *what ifs* when it came to relationships; getting his hopes up almost always ended in disappointment, often through no fault of the other person. So maybe, just maybe, he'd let himself daydream a little about what something more long term with Deacon might look like. It wasn't *only* the explosive, incredible sex or the delightful strangeness of the man himself. And it wasn't *only* the hilariously bad rom-com way they met, and then met again.

He simply liked Deacon. And that was enough for now.

"Mmmm, yeah," Deacon said as he paddled them back down the river. The morning sun was hazy, shrouded by fog rolling off the water and accompanied by the sound of birds greeting the day. "I see it now."

Zan had been studying the way Deacon's arms flexed as he paddled. "Huh...what?"

Deacon chuckled softly. "Just thinking out loud but you got that look on you."

"What, well-laid?"

"Oh sure, boost my ego. I won't argue." Deacon began to slowly navigate a bend in the river, gaze flickering down to the water as a fish jumped near their canoe. "But I mean you look content. It's a good look on you, makes you all relaxed right here." He pointed to the corners of his mouth where deep laugh lines had carved themselves into his skin. "I hope you feel that way all over."

Something vulnerable flickered over Deacon's face. It made Zan want to immediately reassure him, so he said, "Hey, it's all good. We had a hell of a night. And if we weren't in a canoe right now, I'd come over there."

"Really then." The vulnerability in his eyes faded and Deacon's mouth ticked up into a small smile. A warmth bloomed in Zan's chest in response. "Well, all right. So yeah I was thinking second date is on me cause I've got plans. And I feel like my plans and what you like kind of mesh so...hope you don't mind if it's a surprise."

"I'm in your hands." Zan leaned back even further, spreading his thighs just to watch Deacon hone in them like a tracking beam. "Tell me when and where."

When and where was the most ramshackle but utterly charming bookstore Zan had ever seen. "Fawcett Books" was a complete surprise to him, even though it was located only a few towns over in the sleepy seaside port of Fisher's Watch. Sometimes Zan and a few friends would bar hop through the town's main district. They also had a killer teahouse on the outskirts of town. But as he approached the store, Zan realized he'd never really taken the time to explore the town; otherwise, he might have discovered this place on his own. Or, perhaps he *would* have discovered it if it had any kind of name or label on the building itself. The only sign out front of the shop was faded paint that hinted at cream or white but was caked in grime and half-covered by ivy hanging haphazardly over the warped wood and aged brick. The windows were also grimy but the flower boxes clinging to the windowsills were carefully tended and bursting with autumn mums and marigolds. The flowers were the only sign of life outside the building.

Except for Deacon.

He was leaning against the left side of the building, his hands in the pockets of a deep gold and black tweed coat that went down to his knees. There was a bright blue scarf wrapped tightly around Deacon's neck, but his head was bare. The sight of all that black and grey hair made Zan's fingers twitch against his thigh.

Deacon turned his head and thick, dark eyebrows raised over the top of his mirrored aviator sunglasses. "Gorgeous as always, and right on time," Deacon said, pushing away from the wall and immediately pulling Zan to him. "Hi there."

Zan was bursting with questions - what was this store, how did Deacon know about it, where had he gotten that glorious coat - but none of that was as important as being reeled in for a soft kiss. Melting into Deacon's arms felt natural. There was the exciting thrumming of newness in every touch, but they were now days after their first date (and many texts and phone calls and one truly filthy cam call that involved Deacon in and out of leather pants) and it all also felt *good*. Add in that Zan had spent the last several days also working closely with Deacon and his staff over email...well, there was no getting away from the man. And Zan was just fine with such an outcome.

There was also the recognition between them that their lives didn't simply stop because of one epic date. Being in each other's beds all the time wouldn't have been easy to begin with, but they both valued their privacy and respected the boundaries each had drawn. All of that made Zan understand how many of his past dating and relationship partners simply hadn't been on the same page as him.

"Hi." Zan rubbed his thumb over the soft scruff on Deacon's jaw. "Growing a winter beard?"

"Thinking about it." Deacon nuzzled against Zan's hand and pulled him closer. "Are you ready for this? Fawcett's is the town's little secret."

"I have to hear this."

"I'll do one better and show you, yeah?" He pulled a key ring from his pocket and began to unlock the door. Zan wanted to ask so badly but Deacon was clearly excited about his surprise, so Zan let it go. "So head's up. The proprietor is cranky as all get out but there's two cats that will love on you the moment you walk in." Deacon looked up as if assessing something, then said, "Well, one of them might go after you immediately. Bacon's a big fluffy black cat and usually hangs out in the windows to bird watch. Eggs likes the balcony on the second floor so she might be a little slow to come on down."

Zan held up a hand, grinning. "Wait, wait. Those are amazing pet names."

Deacon matched his grin. "I know, right? Especially since they're my cats." He pushed open the door and waved a baffled Zan through.

Darkness lay thick over shelves and shelves...and tables and more shelves packed with books. It was broken up only by sparse yellow sunlight, filtered through both the decorative and clearly antique lead glass windows and a green shaded desk lamp, the kind you operated with a beaded chain and seemed to belong on a noir set.

His eyes didn't feel big enough or sensitive enough to take in *everything*.

Finally, Zan craned his neck to try to get a better view of what was above the switchback stairs in the far-right corner. "Storage, or an office?" he asked, pointing toward the stairs.

Deacon gave a shy smile. *Deacon*. There wasn't anything shy about the man and yet... "I live above. My uncle ran the place back in the eighties and nineties but took an offer from the big bookstore chain that has a district store in Reeder's Wharf. But he loves this place, so I bought it back." He trailed a hand over the closest bookshelf and plucked up a yellowed paperback. "Uncle Benny scoffed at the idea of child labor, so I spent summers here learning to stock and take inventory starting when I was about eleven. Worked here through college, helped build up a clientele. But Uncle Benny didn't want to deal with a store by the time I'd graduated, so he took the money." His mouth turned down, sadness eclipsing his features. Zan squeezed his hand. "Not the kind of shit for a second date. Sorry about that."

"Don't apologize." Zan kissed the corner of his mouth and got a rumble of approval in response. "If this is what you wanted to show me, it's brilliant. Of course I love old bookstores."

"And wine, if I remember right from our chat the morning after the storm."

"Very much so."

Deacon gestured at the store. "It's just us and a big bookstore and a personalized wine tasting. And then, if you're game, a walk down by the pier." His smirk was playful as he lowered his voice and said, "And you're welcome to stay, but I don't expect it. You shared something amazing with me. I thought I'd return the favor."

"Seriously?" This guy was too good to be true and dressed like some kind of model in his tweed coat and cobalt scarf and black hair speckled with gray hanging in his eyes. In the back of his mind, Zan could see that *what if* beginning to crest over the horizon, promising pancakes on Sundays and a bed that was never cold. He shivered and covered it up by tugging on Deacon's lapels, dragging him closer for a kiss. "You're some kind of perfect man conjured up by my lonely imagination, right?"

Sheepish was a good look on Deacon. "Nah, just a guy. Maybe a little lonely. Maybe didn't think that cooling my heels at a skatepark would snare a hottie in black jeans and a peacoat," and Deacon tapped Zan on the nose, "but I ain't about to argue with Fate. She's a little bit of a fickle thing but when you have her favor, you ride that out until the very end."

While Deacon pulled out bottles of wine and tasting boards already stocked with glasses from the large counter that had once been the heart of the store, Zan lingered nearby to browse. "I can't part with all of them yet," Deacon said by way of explanation. "Uncle Benny loved this place and while he was a gruff old bastard, he was always kind to me. Probably not a surprise, I was a weird kid." He flicked hair out of his eyes and grinned. "And grew up to be even weirder. Publishing alien horde orgy books alongside fucking horrifying psychological haunting stories ain't exactly normal."

Zan snorted, pausing his perusal of a dusty bodice-ripper paperback. "But it's certainly a niche. A profitable one."

"No lie, man, if I could run Rochester and just stay afloat, I would do it. But businesses can't run like that."

"And you can't live like that."

A *pop* echoed through the room and Deacon hefted the bottle, examining the label. "True enough. But sometimes it still feels weird." He gestured at the counter and the bottles of wine, as if deflecting. "I'm gonna start pouring, if that's cool."

"Yeah, yeah. But Deacon, you offer a lot of stuff for discount or free. You're doing more than most." Some part of Zan wanted to reassure him, to recite Deacon's publishing strategy (the one listed on Rochester's "Submissions" page, boldly and proudly proclaiming their adherence to freedom to read and be as weird as they wanted). Rochester also helped authors decide when to put certain works on sale, instead of dictating discounts from on high (aka for when it would be most profitable). They were savvy and small enough to maneuver quickly to meet demand. And Rochester did publish fucking weird books, ephemeral and spiritual and dripping in gore or lust or free-wheeling thinking that led a reader down strange, dark alleys.

"And since we're talking books..." Zan dipped his hand into his messenger bag, hand trembling as he set the the advanced copy of Grisolf's newest on the desk. Deacon paused, wine glass in hand, a look of careful expectation on his face. "I ripped through it. And then read it again. It's how I read all of her stuff, once through to immerse myself and then immediately again to take notes." He slid the book to Deacon. "I....you were right. It tops *Ivy and Mercy* in a way I never expected. It's like she stared at the stars too long one night and some mote of the galaxy decided to take up residence in her brain. It's like reading Sagan and Dante and Shirley Jackson all mixed up together." Zan blew out a hard breath and pushed his glasses up his nose. "I feel kind of fucked up."

"Like you took a real nice hallucinogenic trip?"

"Fuck, yeah. I didn't even think of it that way. It was like I could see inside my own brain and sat in the middle of a star all at the same time."

Deacon laughed so hard he had to put the wine glass down. "Oh shit, man. You like....described it perfectly. Can I quote you on that? Yanna would shit herself if she saw a blurb like that."

Zan's brain ground to a halt. "Wait, really?"

"Yeah. She hates everything to do with reviews and all that back-slapping shit but hearing from her readers is her jam." Deacon poured the final glasses and gave a little bow. "So, we should definitely talk about it." But as soon as Zan's ass hit the leather stool, Deacon bolted out of his own. "Hold on! I forgot. Shit...." He dashed up the stairs with a wave, scarf flapping behind him like a streamer.

And that's when Zan met Bacon.

A blur of black fur silently appeared before him like a poofy dark cloud. "Oh, hey there," Zan said. Bacon's bright yellow eyes fixed on him then, in typical cat fashion, he went right for the thing he couldn't have. "Ah, ah, hey buddy, maybe not the wine glasses." Zan put his hand out for Bacon to sniff and that was distraction enough. Soon he was rubbing the cat's silky head and crooning to him in that low voice every human near a cute pet affected. The cat was truly massive, like a small lynx, and had gray facial markings that made him look part puppet.

When Deacon reappeared, he had a covered tray in his hands and a rainbow flag tote bag slung over his shoulder. "I was so focused on the wine I totally spaced. And I see you made a friend." Bacon *mwrowed* softly, a tiny noise for such a large creature, and headbutted Deacon in the bicep. "This one has a head of steel, so watch out. Eggs is upstairs on her second favorite chair, so she's not moving." With a flourish, Deacon uncovered the tray. "Since you liked the picnic spread, I thought I'd put a little twist on it. This is just an appetizer, though. There's an entire pot of stew upstairs. If you want, that is. No pressure, like at all."

Zan smiled over the rim of his glass. Watching Deacon both be in his element and yet slightly nervous was completely charming. Confident guys were fine, but that got old quick because most of them couldn't give up the schtick long enough to be fucking *human*. He was too old to play games, too old to chase, and far too fucking impatient to deal with immaturity. Deacon was several years older, a business owner, a lover of books, adventurous, and a bit (a lot) weird. On paper, they were a good match.

In reality, Zan was seeing how easy it would be to fall for this man. No insta-love here, just a recognition that the spark (and fabulous sex) between them could be even more. That was the kind of excitement he hadn't felt in a long time.

"And the final touch." Soft yellow puddles of light encased them in a warm glow after Deacon removed several battery-operated candles from his tote bag, flipping them on and placing them on the counter. Bacon gave one of them a cursory sniff then sat down on the far end of the counter, tail swishing. "He's standing guard. I think he was a dog in another life."

After a few minutes of quiet, comfortable settling into their food and wine, Deacon reached out to hover his hand over Zan's. "Hey, man, I just wanted to say..." Deacon looked away and sighed heavily. Zan waited him out, watching emotions play across Deacon's face. "Can I?"

Normally Zan's big fucking mouth would let him say something like *well yeah, of course, you've already had your fingers inside me*, but even he realized now wasn't the time. "Sure." He cleared his throat. "I'd love that, actually."

"Okay. Good." Deacon let his hand settle on Zan's before slowly interlinking their fingers. Somewhere in the distance Zan heard a clock ticking. "I wanted you to know that I keep thinking about you and our little cabin adventure." Now Deacon smiled and the candlelight made his piercings and gold tooth glint. "And all the stuff we've talked about and now you're here and I just wanted you to know that it's been nice. Special, in a strange kind of way." He gestured to the bookshop with his free hand. "I don't bring everyone here. And I know I should have just told you that I lived upstairs so it didn't seem like I was springing it on you. Rookie move. But you're here and you didn't run off, so I guess I did all right."

"Deacon." Zan slipped off his stool, pulling Deacon with him. The other man went willingly but his brows were knitted together. Zan couldn't have that. "You are fun and smart and interesting and you press all my fucking buttons. This date? The care you put into everything? Telling me personal stuff about your uncle and this place?" He needed to get his hands on Deacon, to show him beyond a shadow of a doubt that this was all good. More than good; it was right. "Kiss me. Then it's perfect."

And Deacon did.

Once the food was demolished and Bacon given a few nibbles of cheese and ham, they wandered upstairs to polish off their wine. Eggs, Bacon's mirror twin, greeted them with a soft squeak. Deacon held out his arms and she leapt into them. "Holy shit, they really are like dogs," Zan said as he focused on the cat instead of peering around at Deacon's place. "Hello, sweetie."

Eggs squeaked again and they both laughed. "I think that's her hello," Deacon replied before nuzzling against the cat's head. Eggs let out a rumbling purr before jumping down, intent on brushing up against Zan's legs, tail high in the air. He let her sniff his hand then take the bit of cheese he'd tucked away in his palm.

Deacon gave a theatrical gasp. "Bribing *my cats*? Now who's the scoundrel."

Well, in for a...penny, farthing, whatever. Zan quickly straightened, leaned in, and kissed Deacon hard. His tongue begged for entrance against Deacon's lips and the man didn't hold back. His soft groan rattled through Zan, made him grab and grip. Deacon's hair was soft, the springy waves of it almost tangling around his fingers of their own regard and when he pulled a little, Deacon muttered, "Fuck. Zan."

"Too much, *old man*?"

The challenge was met with a heady, dark look from Deacon. Zan shivered. "Try me." He pulled Zan further into the apartment by the hand then kissed the back of it. "Tour first?"

Now Zan gave the place a proper look around and he saw it. The puzzle pieces of Deacon were clicking into place. Upon meeting the man it would be easy to expect his home to be full of interesting or odd things. There were some items on shelves that caught his eye - resin sculptures that looked almost like carnival masks, stacks and stacks of books that were neatly organized and displayed between concrete bookends, random glinting bric-a-brac that begged to be inspected. And the entire space was lined in the kind of bare brick and old hardwood floors that most people would kill a family member for. But despite the beautiful space, it was clear Deacon liked a clean home; even with two cats and tons of old books, Zan saw no pet hair floating about or smelled anything outside of hints of coffee and a bit of fresh air from the balcony door.

And speaking of the balcony...Zan now tugged Deacon over and said, "Wow. The view." From here, they could see all the way to the boardwalk, where little figures moved about as the waves gently licked against the shore.

"The view." Deacon grinned before nuzzling close, his arm snug around Zan's waist. It was impossible to not lean in as well, if only to feel Deacon's stubble against his cheek. Movement at his ankles saw Bacon brushing up against them both, head turned up to focus those yellow eyes as if to ask what they were doing. "Even if this hadn't been Uncle Benny's place, I would have bought it for the view alone."

Zan swallowed hard. "Hadn't been?"

That got him a chuckle. "Ol' Benny's busy spending his retirement years sailing. It's wild, the guy's in his seventies and he has the energy of a college kid. I think retirement did right by him. He stops back around from time to time, mostly to check that I haven't burned the place down or anything."

"Once someone's nephew, always someone's nephew, huh?"

"Especially when said nephew used to have a thing for fire. Can't blame the guy." Deacon let out the kind of quiet sigh that spoke to silent depths Zan wasn't going to plumb - too personal, too close to the chest - but the wind carried the sound away from them, out over the sidewalks and buildings and out, maybe, to the ocean beyond. "So, you've been in the place. You know the story. What's say we get back to what we were doing?"

Like Zan could resist that. "Talking about books?"

Deacon pinched his side. "If you want. I thinking more in terms of activities that involved nudity."

"You scoundrel." Zan backed up a step so he could tip his chin up and give Deacon a look he hoped was enticing. "Show me the way."

NINE

Deacon's bedroom was all blues and yellow and orange patterns, beautifully laid out across a rectangular space big enough for the massive bed in the middle. And the man himself wasted no time in kissing his way down Zan's jaw and neck, hands roaming everywhere.

"Take it off." The quiet command made something deep inside Zan shiver with anticipation.

"You first."

Deacon slapped his ass, making Zan jolt. Little tendrils of pleasure flickered through him. Deacon certainly had a way of making him discover new things about his own desires. *Challenging, fascinating man.* "Same time, then."

In Zan's haste to get his clothes off, he'd forgotten the two buttons inside his cowled sweater; the ones meant to keep the ends from flapping in the wind. But now one was snagged in his hair and he was hopelessly stuck. "Save me?" he pleaded, batting his eyes at Deacon through the bottom of his sweater.

Deacon was doing an admirable job of not laughing, but he did cross his arms over his bare chest. Which sadly had the effect of hiding some of his tattoos and his nipple rings. "Ask nicely, handsome." He edged closer, tongue darting out to wet his lips as he looked Zan over. "And we can discuss Grisolf *after*. I bet it'll be surprisingly good pillow talk, yeah?"

Zan could imagine it easily. The two of them curled up to face each other as their tacky skin cooled and their hearts slowed to normal. Deacon's hair would be gorgeously mussed and he'd be unable to keep his fingers out of it, combing through snarls until Deacon had drifted off.

"Yeah," he said through a tight throat, doing his best to hide it. Deacon seemed pleased with his answer and tone, but Zan felt that *what if* creeping up again. Rearing its head to waggle a potential future in front of his eyes as if to say, "See what you could have if you don't fuck it up?"

Zan turned away and wriggled inside his sweater once more before Deacon took pity on him. And with the sweater discarded, Deacon wasted no time in running his hands under Zan's thin t-shirt. "Gonna have a hard time forgetting the sight of you in my bed," he purred, thumbs skating over Zan's nipples. Melting into Deacon's touch, his embrace, was as easy as tipping his head up for a kiss.

When those kisses were interspersed with ragged moans and heavy breathing, Deacon all but danced them over to the bed. "I thought you couldn't dance," Zan said against Deacon's lips.

"This is...bedroom dancing. It's different."

Zan pulled back and gave him a look. "I swear to god if you say it's the horizontal mambo, I'm leaving."

Deacon laughed until he was red in the face and Zan was laughing with him and then they were tumbling onto the bed and kissing again, clinging to each other.

God, it really was this easy, wasn't it? If this didn't work out, disappointment would be an understatement. He *liked* Deacon. Zan liked the way Deacon moaned under his touch, writhing to get closer; the way his smile curled up at the edges (but a little higher on the right). He liked the way they fit and even now, as they fumbled and swore and laughed at how stupid but how good the sex was, Zan could feel his heart pounding under that heady, shimmering promise of *what if*.

And when Deacon entered him from behind, the angle and piercings making his eyes roll back and his breath escape like he'd been punched, he was helpless in watching Deacon weave their fingers together.

Deacon kept him right at the edge for several long moments, maybe minutes even. Zan could feel the fire in his gut beg for release...and then Deacon would pull back and drag those piercings through him. He felt like screaming, like pleading, but all Zan could do was grip the headboard and try to bear down, to tease in his own way with what strength he had left.

"Fuckin' hell, Zan. Look at us." Deacon squeezed Zan's hands tighter as he thrust hard. Zan groaned and shivered and felt some strange connection building between them - their bodies, their hands, their breaths.

His head swimming, Zan turned into Deacon's touch as Deacon pressed forward until his lips were on Zan's ear. "Look at..." Deacon squeezed their hands together again. "Look at that. Good fit."

"*Deacon*, I - ah, god -"

Deacon shifted again, driving into him harder, deeper. Everything became a blur. The heat, the sweat, the pleasure all swirled within him and Zan cried out. There were foggy points of focus - Deacon's hands on his, the way they were plastered together, how Deacon's cock felt inside him. But he was *so close* and that little push over the edge was just out of reach. He wanted to sob, to rip his hand away and stroke himself. It happened sometimes like this - him pushed all the way to the cliff's edge but unable to come, growling in frustration at his own body's reticence.

"I got you." Reassurance lay heavy in Deacon's words. "Hold on."

"Deacon, fuck." Another drag of Deacon's cock inside him brought him closer. *More, more. Please more. Keep doing whatever fucking genius thing that is because I'm so close...*

"I know." Whatever Deacon did, some magic shift of his hips or maybe tensing his muscles, it lit sparks behind Zan's eyes. "Want me to touch you?"

Zan's *yes* was more of a desperate grunt, but Deacon didn't tease him. He simply let his right hand drop. Once those warm, callused fingers met his overheated skin, Zan nearly jolted in relief. He was *right there*, just *a little more...*

"I'm close," Deacon panted in his ear. "But I wanna fuck you when you come. Feel you clench down on me."

"Goddammit." Zan pressed back against Deacon's rolling, hypnotic thrusts.

"Good. Good boy."

Deacon had his cock in a tight grip and that felt *so fucking right*. But what did it was the hard, sharp edge of a nail in his slit. Pleasure soaked every nerve, every follicle. Zan was aware of everything and nothing at the same time, barely able to hear Deacon's little words of praise. And getting fucked raw as he came made everything hurt in the perfect kind of way.

"What's this?" Zan took the sheet of paper from Deacon's outstretched hand.

"Plans for a party. Just a small one." Deacon waggled his eyebrows at Zan before flopping into bed and immediately pulling him close. "Yanna wants to do a book signing. And me and Trina, who owns Phoenix Books just up the road, are good friends. Yanna likes the place so..." He waved his hand in the air. "Small book signing, bit of a talk with those gathered. Thinking we'll do an exclusive hardcover, limited run, and then paperbacks for regular stock on our site and with the indies."

Once Rucker got wind of an *exclusive, limited-run hardback*, he'd cream himself. Oakside almost always printed paperbacks for its customers; larger paper wasn't cheap, for one, and binding hardbacks sometimes doubled the costs. Immediately, Zan started doing the math in his head. Maybe they could finally buy a new conference room table.

"...and maybe some bookmarks. Flyers, course, to advertise the event. My marketing head, Phen, has all that stuff handled." Zan had zoned out while Deacon talked and the man either didn't notice or didn't care. When Zan glanced over, Deacon had his head pillowed on his bicep and was grinning Zan's way. "I saw the cogs turning. Adding up the cash, yeah?"

Shit. "Rucker's gonna love it. Staying ahead of him is half my job."

"Seems like an...interesting man to work for."

Zan snorted, choosing to focus on the feel of Deacon's leg between his instead of his love/dislike relationship with his boss. *Hate* was too strong a word, of course; he didn't hate anyone but often could harbor a deep loathing for the occasional malicious asshole. Working with Rucker was like sitting across a picnic or holiday table from the uncle with permanent foot-in-mouth disease. Zan had settled into a steady set of routines at work that had not only made his job easier but had kept Rucker at arm's length. It was his crutch, but a necessary one.

"Hey, I'm not about to make your job harder with all this. Besides, now that I have a reliable printer, we can both help each other out." Something soft stole over Deacon's face and it helped Zan ease some of the tension out of his spine. "I ain't here to be a bother, hot stuff."

"I don't think those who are trying to be bothersome let me into their apartment and then fuck me stupid."

Now Deacon laughed. He really, really did have a nice one. It settled over Zan comfortably, like the soft duvet they'd snuggled into. "Was it that good?"

"You know it was."

Deacon gave him the kind of smile that might split a lesser man in two.

Well, Zan was just fine with being a lesser man, for all the ways that very smile made him feel.

Ten

Two weeks, four more dates, and a few nights spent in Deacon's bed later

"Holy shit, man, it smells amazing in here." Deacon turned a full circle in Zan's foyer. The space was barely big enough to be called a foyer, since it was just a hallway off the front door that led into the main body of his home. But he'd had enough people over for dinner or parties over the years to know the place was undeniable in its funky way. "But also...this is a Van Alsden. It's *the* Van Alsden everyone said was outside town but you couldn't see from the road."

"Long driveways back into the woods are good for that." Zan swept his gaze up to the curved white ceilings and hive-like structures that clung to the walls and perched in the corners. "Dad always wanted the inside to be impressive and the outside unassuming."

Deacon wore a stunned expression, taking a few steps forward before remembering himself and immediately toeing off his brown leather boots. When he reapproached Zan, it was with that same stunned expression, but now something in those brown eyes was calculating. "Wait. Wait. Zan."

And then Deacon started laughing. Not cruelly or even in disbelief, but in utter *joy*. It threw Zan for a loop. "Want to let me in on the joke?"

Deacon actually had a hand on his chest, he was laughing so hard. "Your dad...oh *fuck*, hold up, I need a moment. Fuck me." He heaved a few comically dramatic breaths. "Okay, okay...your *dad* was Leopold Van Alsden? *The* Leo Van Alsden that created some of the most beautiful house interiors I've ever seen? That anyone's ever seen? And you just so happen to live in his *masterpiece*?"

Zan's throat went dry, his heart hammering a little harder. Memories of his dad had long faded to the quiet, dull things but every now and then they'd hit like a one-two from a heavyweight champion. He'd become accustomed to living in *Hive House* and seeing his dad in the slowly growing cracks along the house's creases and in the mossy flagstone paths that wound around the backyard. But Deacon's sheer delight in putting a few pieces of him together left Zan feeling a little dizzy.

"It's a long story," he said quietly. "But yeah."

And then Deacon was standing in front of him, soft expectation over his sharp, rugged features. "It's brilliant is what it is." His eyes flicked to the right, to the honeycomb patterns burned into the wood beams and the three-legged table where Zan put his keys and wallet and had propped up several framed pictures. "I get to see more of you now. More *you*. More than the Zan who bosses people around or who makes bad jokes or sometimes runs his mouth a bit."

There was no denying the smirk that stole over his features. "Just a bit? It *is* good for other things, too."

"Maybe later," Deacon said, running his fingertip along Zan's jaw, "we can talk about running it a little more." And he whirled away, leaving Zan to shake his head and laugh. "Oh fuck man, you should see the look on your face. Like I just took away your favorite toy."

"You did," he shot back as he led Deacon into the airy kitchen. More white walls and deep golden oak beams lined the space. In the middle of the kitchen was the tiled island his father had crafted with his own hands. Zan had memories of handing his dad the tiles, hexagon after white and blue hexagon that slowly became more than something lodged firmly in Leo's imagination. And by now, that island had hosted parties and dinners and been the center of a lot more memories. It sat gleaming in the late morning light, packed with ingredients for the brunch he'd promised Deacon as a way to celebrate successfully printing the first batch of Yanna Grisolf hardcovers.

Deacon continued to stare, slightly awestruck, while Zan began uncovering bowls of pre-chopped vegetables. "This is...damn. Can't believe your dad was Leo Van Alsden." He looked down and shoved his hands in his pockets. "Sorry, you probably get that a lot."

"It's okay. Honestly..." Zan sighed, hand hovering over the pan he needed to move to the flat top stove. "Every time someone oohs and aahs over the house, it's like getting to share a little piece of him. It's nice. I *used* to hate it but that was grief talking. Time does funny things to you after you lose someone."

"Shit yeah it does." Deacon tapped the side of his head. "Fucked me up a long time ago. I get you, really."

While Zan shuffled all the bowls and pans around to make his epic garden vegetable omelet, Deacon watched him over the rim of a dark blue coffee mug. The steam curled in front of his face and occasionally obscured his features, leaving Zan with only glimpses of thick, dark eyebrows and the glint of piercings.

Eventually, Deacon said, "So hey, wanted to ask you something. And I'm hoping you'll be honest with me on this, cause I'm too old to play games."

Zan paused, hand on the whisk beside a bowl full of eggs. Something like dread unfurled in his stomach. "Okay."

Deacon set his coffee cup down but didn't let go of it, choosing to wrap both hands around its warmth. It was vulnerable in some way Zan couldn't quite parse. "So, truth time here, yeah? I like you, Zan. And I think you maybe feel the same, or maybe could get there. But I've never thrown myself at people and if you don't feel the way I do, then I'm thinking we go back to just business. I ain't about to hold a grudge against Oakside or anything -"

"Deacon."

"And the thing is, at first I thought it was cause you could keep up with my mind." He twirled a finger near his temple. "Cartwheels up here, sometimes. Like drunken hamster cartwheels."

"*Deacon.*" Zan let the whisk drop to the counter and took two big steps to the right, big enough so he could quickly press into Deacon's space. Deacon immediately snapped his mouth shut, his brown eyes flared wide.

Vulnerable

That word, that sensation beat between them like another heart. It hovered over Zan's hands as he took Deacon's and squeezed their fingers together. "Deacon. I feel the same way. We fit nicely together. I don't want to 'go back to just business'. I want to keep seeing each other." He leaned in and Deacon did too, their lips close enough to brush but didn't. Not quite, not yet. "We keep learning new things about each other. I like getting to know you." He let a smirk crawl across his face. "And it's certainly the best sex I've had in...nope, actually, ever. Ever. The best sex I've ever had."

That got Deacon to chuckle. Zan had discovered over these last few weeks that Deacon really liked having his bedroom talents praised, almost as much as Zan liked being praised for *taking Deacon*. It was a feedback loop in a strange, sensual way. But it worked for them.

"So, we're doing this thing?"

"Yeah." Zan smiled at Deacon. "Didn't think I'd get so cheesy about someone so quickly."

"Hey, I like cheesy." Deacon's grin matched Zan's. "Our first date ended with sex in an abandoned cabin while it poured buckets. Doesn't get much cheesier than that."

After brunch and just the right number of mimosas, Zan led Deacon back to the study. "My favorite spot," he said as Deacon slowly walked around the brightly lit room. The study sat on the back of the house and received the morning sun; combined with the high, sloping walls and golden oak floors and beams, the entire space felt both open and cozy. And Zan, being the nester he was, had thrown blankets and pillows on both burnished pumpkin chaise lounges with more folded up in a basket nearby.

"Care to relive our childhoods?" he asked, gesturing to the drafting table in the middle of the room.

Deacon's eyes widened, taking in the basket of pencils, the stack of papers and well-loved hardcover books with all the little flags marking their pages. Then to the multi-hued miniatures scattered about the table. "No way."

"Care for a Dungeon Delve session?"

One moment, Zan's feet were firmly on the ground and the next, Deacon had lifted him up in a hug that crushed his ribs and expanded his heart at least four times. "You are the fucking *best*," Deacon rumbled in his ear. "Brunch was more than enough but this?" He pulled back to rest his forehead against Zan's. They breathed against each other and Zan couldn't help but feel warm all over.

There was something about Deacon that made him wonder, and he liked that.

"Glad you like it."

"Man, I don't know where you came from but if you keep doing shit like this? Yeah, I'm never leaving."

Zan ran his fingertips across Deacon's cheek, then down to his lips. He didn't have the words right now, but he hoped his touch conveyed enough. "Then let's do this," he replied instead.

They spent the afternoon huddled over the drafting table, moving miniatures and dungeon tiles across its scratched surface. The first three rounds were always the toughest to survive; when your heroes were low level and equipped with the basic armor from the character creation tables. Deacon lost a wizard and an assassin and Zan nearly wiped out the entire party by accidentally setting off a trap. When he was a kid, he would have argued tooth and nail against the exact determination of the trap's blast radius and that his warrior wouldn't have been in range to receive damage - like a true nerd. But now, as an adult reliving memories and getting to spend the day with someone he really liked, Zan found the game relaxing. The minis were just cheap things, their painted features faded; the dungeon tiles were obviously well-used, their corners dinged and worn. And his Dungeon Delve books cracked with age as pages were turned.

But he loved every minute, and so did Deacon.

When another trap let Deacon cast a countering spell, they both cheered like they were ten and in a dimly lit basement after school, discarded snack wrappers and soda bottles around them. It was magnetic, that moment; when Zan turned to see Deacon grinning at him, he wrapped his arm around the other man's neck and pulled him for a kiss.

"You're the fucking *best*," Deacon murmured against his mouth. Zan clutched him tighter in response. "And if this wasn't your place but mine, I'd scatter all that stuff on the table with one big sweep of my hand."

Zan swallowed hard. He could *see* it, the grand gesture, the hot anticipation in Deacon's eyes. Kind of like how Deacon was staring at him now. "And then?"

There was something a tiny bit feral in Deacon's grin, helped along by the glint of gold. "I'd bend you over the table and watch you scrabble for purchase as I yank your jeans down."

Zan breathed out a curse, swallowed hard. "And?"

"Greedy thing." Deacon trailed his fingertips over Zan's cheek, light as air. "What would you want?"

Zan was gripping Deacon's shirt so hard now that some part of him worried he'd rend the fabric. "You need me to tell you?"

"Yes. Yes, I fucking do. Because you are so fun to give to and I'd do anything-"

"Then fuck me."

"Now?" Deacon looked amused, his smile crinkling the corners of his eyes. "Here? After we just beat the big boss's trap?" Zan was ready to fire back, snipe at him, beg him for *anything*.

And then Deacon dropped his voice and trailed his touch down Zan's neck. "Before I drop to my knees and lick you open?"

Maybe he whimpered, or maybe Deacon was finally giving in, but Zan was able to crush his mouth against Deacon's for a split second before snapping, "Bedroom's down the hall."

"I love the way you think." Deacon leaned in to nose against Zan's throat. "And the way you beg."

Eleven

Around eight pm the night of the Yanna Grisolf signing

The evening had, so far, gone off without a hitch. Phoenix Books and Rochester Press pulled out all the stops, from the planning to marketing to the food and event set-up. The store practically lent itself to intimate readings and other events, with its polished cherry shelves, slightly creaking floors, and second story jammed with plaid armchairs and low-slung velvet couches. Classic, in a "your dad's smoking den sans the smoke" kind of way.

But everything had really been a blur since tickets sold out in mere minutes for Yanna's signing, and pre-orders had broken a store - and a publisher - record. It was no longer a Rochester event, with Zan and company off to the side printing the books. It became a joint event. And while convincing Rucker to pony up some money to add to the event funds had been a hard sell, his pitch for increased revenue and reputation had been the deal breaker.

Now the big night had arrived, and the crowd had started filing in an hour ago. Zan had made sure that Oakside staff were there to help, but he was at Deacon's side all night. The number of grateful looks

Deacon had shot him as the time of Yanna's live reading drew near had made all the hustle and stress worth it.

And yet Zan couldn't help but feel a strange sensation, off-putting and almost sour on his tongue. Everything had gone so smoothly, so surely there was some hitch. In the background, he was beyond excited to finally meet Yanna Grisolf but he couldn't shake that pessimistic feeling. *You're being you,* he thought blithely. *Knock it off.*

"You ready?"

Zan quelled the urge to jump out of his skin, but it was a near thing. "Holy shit," he hissed as Deacon chuckled beside him. "You're like a ninja."

"A very sexy one though, yeah?"

Zan looked him over - black suit, dark red shirt open a little too much (*or just the right amount*), and bright yellow topaz earrings. Deacon looked polished in that slightly ruffled kind of way. Except Deacon managed it with no effort other than being himself.

It made Zan want to lick him, damn everyone around them.

"Zan?"

"Extremely sexy," he replied. "And a very good thing we're at the back of this crowd that's forming because otherwise, everyone would be getting a show."

Deacon chuckled, the sound warm and inviting. Promising rumpled covers and linked fingers. "I'll remember to explore that later." When Zan gave him a confused look, Deacon said, "Exhibitionist," kissed him on the cheek, and then slipped through the crowd to hold open the shop's door. Zan looked at the floor and hoped no one saw him bite his lip.

The hush that fell over everyone gathered for the event was palpable, settling on Zan's skin like the air in a church. Trina, the owner of the bookstore, was leading Yanna Grisolf through the front door. She gave Deacon a bright smile, then waved in the author. People were used to how she looked in interviews - a cross between Stevie Nicks and Bea Arthur, with a throaty smoker's voice to match. But tonight, apparently Yanna had pulled out all the stops, too. Zan heard someone say, "Holy shit," as the silver sequined lapels on her purple tuxedo caught the light.

Yanna surveyed the crowd, squinted, then let out a laugh. "That's a lot of fucking people, Deacon. Goddamn."

The bubble of silence burst and everyone laughed. Deacon was all smiles now, slinging an arm out for Yanna to take as he escorted her over to the massive table where piles of her newest book awaited. Yanna was smiling now as well, her dark eyes lighting up as people waved and clapped. And while the crowd watched Yanna, Zan kept looking at Deacon.

His favorite author of all time in the room with the man who was slowly, one date at a time, changing his world. *What if* was quietly becoming something a little else. And for the first time Zan could remember, that didn't make him nervous or scared. Nervous for things to progress, scared that he was moving too fast. He wasn't getting any younger and while he didn't hang onto nascent platitudes about how "age is just a number", Zan knew each passing year taught him some things. To stop mouthing off so much, to be a little more optimistic. To take chances, shove a middle finger at the rules.

There were no rules for whatever was building between him and Deacon. He *liked that*. It was exciting. *Deacon* was exciting.

Zan looked up and locked eyes with Deacon. Deacon waved, then pointed in his direction to Yanna. *Oh god.*

With a deep breath, Zan walked through the crowd and up to the front. Someone near him grumbled but Deacon said, "There he is! Zan is why your books look so fucking good, Yanna."

Those canny brown eyes hit him with the full force of Yanna's gaze and Zan felt his stomach flutter a little. "Then clearly the first book off the stack should be his." With a flick of her hand, Yanna opened the front cover (shit, that had been his job, to hand her the books already opened to the right page), scrawled something inside, then shut the book and handed it to him. "Deacon says you're a fan," she replied as he took the signed copy of *Tender, Wild Mercies*. "And you provided that blurb for the back. I'm honored. I'd rather a reader tell me the truth any day over some reviewer bullshit blowing smoke up my ass."

One part of his brain slowed to a crawl, but his mouth didn't forget how to move. "You probably hear this all the time," Zan said quickly, trying so hard not to gush. "But *Philosophy of Ivy and Mercy* changed me. I can't thank you enough for that."

That canny gaze was back, but it was softened by a small smile. "Can I ask you something, Zan?"

"Yes, ma'am."

She sniffed but didn't correct or tease him. "How did it change you?"

Zan locked eyes with Deacon, who was hovering near Yanna's right shoulder. He had given this a lot of thought, since every yearly reading brought him something new, or at least a new path to ponder. "Not all at once, or in some grand revelation. It made me pause. That wasn't something I'd really done before. It taught me to value the quiet spaces between thoughts, or breaths." And out of the messenger bag he'd been wearing all night, Zan pulled out his incredibly well-used, clearly well-loved copy of that same book. He watched Yanna look down at the yellowed pages, the dog earned corners, the sticky flags hanging out at all angles. Her eyes traveled over the creased, cracked cover. No judgment, no smile, but a nod. A nod of understanding.

"Do you want me to sign it?" Yanna asked, sliding her finger along the worn edge. "A book like this deserves to be signed. There's love here, and heartbreak. And I'm grateful to you for both."

All Zan could manage was a quiet, "Please."

After she'd signed with a flourish and Zan relayed his thanks, he put both books away in his bag and took up Deacon's space while the other man went to help with the line. As Deacon passed, he squeezed Zan's shoulder. "Good man."

"Deacon." Deacon paused and looked back at Yanna, who simply said, "For fuck's sake, man, just kiss him."

And since she said it in front of everyone, the crowd cheered.

"Are we going to kiss in front of a crowd?" Zan teased. "That's pretty close to as cheesy as our first date."

Deacon drew close, said, "Is it, now?", and kissed him.

As the party wound down, Zan finally found a moment to enjoy a glass of wine with Deacon and be able to say more than two words to Teny and Rucker. Both uncle and nephew had been at the party right on time, but Rucker had managed to work the floor like the charming salesman he was, while Teny had stuck to the outskirts, chatting with a few folks here and there. Zan had no complaints about either, but he'd felt a twinge of regret seeing Teny alone on the sidelines so much. Especially while Rucker had been running his damn mouth all night except for when Yanna did her reading.

Hoping Rucker was losing steam this late at night, Zan steered Deacon over to his boss. Rucker made the usual pleasantries, then (much to Zan's shock), loudly proclaimed, "What an event! Incredible! We sold more books than ever -"

"I thought that was my line," Deacon rumbled in his ear.

" - and it's all thanks to the best print shop manager. Proud of you, Zan." Rucker clapped him on the shoulder.

Holy shit, that might be actual gratitude. From his boss.

"Uh, thanks, Rucker. But it was a group effort."

"To his credit, Rucker, Zan isn't one for boasting. I, however, very much am and I know for a fact that without Zan, those books would have never been printed so quickly." Deacon's reply was smooth, but his brown eyes spoke volumes, especially the little crinkles at their corners.

And the hand running down Zan's back, fingertips bumping along his spine, told another story.

"True, all true," Rucker said, nodding, his dark hair flopping with the movement. "Well, hell of a night. Hell of a night! I just gotta grab Teny -"

They all turned to the corner Teny had propped himself up in and saw him talking to a person in a bright yellow dress, several dark braids laying over their shoulders. Both looked utterly absorbed in their conversation. "Might want to leave him be," Zan told Rucker, whose brow had gone pinched. "He looks a little busy."

"He knows how to call for a car, Rucker," Deacon added, and Zan shot him a silent look of gratitude. The fingers on his back tapped out a one-two rhythm, like a lover's Morse code.

"Right. Right. Well, guess I'll be off."

Zan and Deacon both said their goodbyes and Rucker made his way to the front of the store. "I thought he'd never leave," Zan sighed with relief, making Deacon laugh. "Jesus fuckin' A, that man..."

"Is coming right back so laugh like I said something funny."

"Shit uh..." Zan laughed, the sound forced, and Deacon held back a snort just in time for Rucker to round on them. "Rucker!"

"Sorry, sorry. Just remembered, what was the name of those rain boots you'd recommended, Zan?" Rucker now looked agitated, but Zan was pretty sure it wasn't because he'd overheard Zan's bad-mouthing. "I gotta get out to the woods this weekend and it's supposed to rain."

Flabbergasted, Zan said, "Wait, the AllTechs?"

"That was it!" Rucker snapped his fingers. "I know, I know. I don't usually head out that way, but the old family cabin's been standing alone too long and I figured it was time to start clearing it out." Just as something wiggled in the back of Zan's mind and he started to ask, "Cabin?", Rucker leaned into both of them and loudly whispered, "You know, some assholes broke in a few weeks back? I must have just missed them, cause the food they left was in the outdoor trash cans. Thank fuck for that, at least. But I think they *slept in the bed!* And fucked in it!" Rucker's already ruddy face turned another shade of tomato. "Christ, no one's got any fuckin' manners anymore! I get it looks abandoned and I might have let it go a little..."

"A lot," Deacon said, getting a sharp elbow from Zan. The fucker's smile was so big, Zan swore they were busted.

But Rucker did as he was wont to and kept rambling. "Yeah, okay, I haven't really kept it up at all! But breaking and entering! Fucking in someone else's bed! It's just....well, it's uncivilized." And with that, Rucker deflated. "Right, AllTech boots. Got it. Thanks, Zan."

And then he was gone again, humming loudly and waving goodbye to Trina.

Silence filled the space between he and Deacon.

"Don't say it," Zan warned, but he could hear the laughter bubbling up in Deacon's chest. "Fuck. Oh, fuck."

"Oh my *god*..."

"Deacon."

"*Holy shit, Zan.*"

"Deacon!"

Deacon threw his head back and laughed, hand on his chest, eyes squeezed shut as tears of mirth ran down his face. "We fucked in your boss's cabin!"

Two months later

"Ow."

"Aw, that just means he loves you."

His arm stung from where Bacon had headbutted it, but Zan reached out to scratch at the cat's fluffy ears. "Brute."

Deacon snickered as he walked over to deposit more pancakes on Zan's plate. "Want any more?"

"Ugh, no. Have mercy." Zan put a hand on his stomach. "I'm gonna have to run laps as it is. I feel like I've swallowed a beach ball."

"Pretty hot for a beach ball, babe." Deacon pressed a kiss to his cheek, then settled on the stool beside him, ignoring Zan's playful grumbling. "You know, there are other ways to burn off the pancakes."

A wave of heat rushed through him. "Deacon. I literally cannot do that again after this morning. I thought you were gonna split me in half."

With a toothy grin, Deacon wiggled his eyebrows. "I didn't hear any complaining. And besides, you woke me up at five in the morning with a raging boner." He leaned in and licked maple syrup from the corner of Zan's mouth. "Like I was gonna ignore that."

"You are terrible."

"Pretty much." Deacon's warm fingers were on his, those dark eyes dancing with mischief. "Again, never heard any complaining."

"Okay so, if not sex, then what?"

"We take the cats for a walk."

Zan chewed on his pancakes and gave Bacon a sideways glance. "You said they have to trust the person walking them. You think we're ready?"

Deacon burst out laughing and Zan turned to see Bacon swiping a whole pancake from Zan's plate. "I think we're more than good."

"Fucker stole my pancake."

"Yep!"

Bacon took off, trailing pancake crumbs and maple syrup across the floor and Deacon bolted after him. "Wait, Deacon! Let him have it!"

All three skidded around the corner, Bacon in the lead, while Deacon and Zan gave chase, laughing the entire way across the apartment. When Bacon slipped under the bed, his prize now out of reach, Deacon collapsed on top of the bed and laughed into the pillows. "That is the smartest cat I've ever seen," Zan said as he flopped down beside Deacon. "Eggs doesn't care a single bit about human food. And then there's *him*."

"You don't care, do you lovey?" Deacon craned his head to stare at Eggs, who was fast asleep in their abandoned blankets. "She just wants blankets and head scratches."

Turning on his side, Zan grinned down at Deacon. "And what if I want blankets and head scratches?"

Deacon immediately crooked a finger at him. "Then come here."

"Yeah?"

"Course." They moved around until Deacon was propped up against some pillows and Zan was able to lay in his lap, head cradled between Deacon's strong hands and his legs stretched out across the bed. "How's that?"

"Magical." Zan closed his eyes and groaned. Deacon's fingers were magic, rubbing soft circles into his scalp and combing through his hair. "I love this."

"I know you do."

This is insane, Zan thought. *Who says I love you after a few months?* But then again, who cared?

Shimmering warmth covered him, a sweet, welcome sensation on the back of that realization. Because the only people who could care were him and Deacon. That was all that mattered. The *whens* and *hows* were up to them, like every other part of their relationship.

"You're very good to me," Zan whispered as he looked up at Deacon, watching the way Deacon's smile washed over his face. It was a nice face, with its deep laugh lines and piercings and thick brows. "I think I'm..." His throat tightened. Something hot flashed in his chest, some surge of emotion he had no name for. "I might be falling for you."

Deacon's fingers stilled and those eyes (*damn those eyes*) bored into him. Panic fluttered in his belly and Zan started to speak again, but Deacon said, "And here I thought I'd be the first one to admit it. Huh."

Realization was a heavy thing, an anvil on his lungs. "Deacon?"

Deacon leaned forward and kissed Zan's forehead. Then the bridge of his nose. Then, lips hovering over Zan's, Deacon whispered, "Love's a funny thing, yeah? Gets us all bound up but really, it's the fucking best."

Under the bed, Bacon let out a soft *mrrow* and they both laughed until they couldn't breathe. "The best," Zan managed to say as he pulled Deacon into another kiss.

THE END

ACKNOWLEDGMENTS

Many thanks to my beta and early readers. Folks like Agu, Alex, and Cayla are big cheerleaders, yes, but also willing to provide feedback – in any shape or size. Any writer worth their salt knows the value of good – critical – feedback.

ABOUT AUTHOR

Halli Starling (she/they) is a queer author, librarian, gamer, editor, and nerd. When He Beckons is her fourth book. Her work can be found on hallistarlingbooks .com and she's on Twitter and Instagram @hallistarling.

Made in the USA
Monee, IL
13 May 2023